Those who can not remember the past are condemned to repeat it.
(George Santayana)

THE LAWMEN

BY ALTON PRYOR

Stagecoach Publishing
5360 Campcreek Loop
Roseville, CA 95747
916-771-8166
stagecoach@surewest.net
www.stagecoachpublishing.com

The Lawmen

Copyright © Alton Pryor 2006

Library of Congress Control Number 2005909053

ISBN: 0-9747551-6-8

First Printing 2006

Stagecoach Publishing
5360 Campcreek Loop
Roseville, CA. 95747
(916) 771-8166
stagecoach@surewest.net
www.stagecoachpublishing.com

Table of Contents

This photo depicts some of the West's most well-known lawmen. Seated, left to right, are Charles E. Bassett, Wyatt Earp, M.C. Clark and Neil Brown. Standing, W.H. Harris, Luke Short and Bat Masterson. (Kansas Historical Society)

CHAPTER I

WYATT EARP

'He wasn't always the gentleman'

In legend, Wyatt Earp shot straight, waded into the worst of outlaws and walked on water.

Some historians claim the Earp legend too often veered from truth. Often, it was Earp himself that gave rise to the false impression.

The start of the legend began at Ellsworth, Kansas, where Earp claimed to have disarmed Ben Thompson, a Texas gambler that was considered one of the frontier's most deadly gunfighters.

Records show that Earp wasn't even there. Still, the legend lives on.

Wyatt Earp
1848-1929
(Google Images)

Wyatt Berry Stapp Earp was born in Monmouth, Illinois on March 19, 1848. In 1864, he moved with his parents to Colton, California in San Bernardino County. There, he was employed as a teamster and as a railroad worker.

11

Wyatt returned east in 1870 and married his first wife, Urilla Sutherland. His new wife lived but a short time. There are two reported versions of her cause of death. One is that she died of typhus. The other is that she died in childbirth.

Wyatt later ran against his older half-brother Newton for the constable's post. Wyatt won, getting one-hundred thirty seven votes to Newton's one-hundred-eight votes. This would be the only time Earp would run for office.

After his wife's death, Wyatt began having troubles with the law. Barton County, Missouri filed a lawsuit again Earp, charging him with failure to deliver the license fees he collected for the town of Lamar, Missouri. The fees were for funding for local schools. The action was eventually vacated, most likely because he had left the state.

After that, Wyatt drifted through Indian Territory, working as a buffalo hunter and stagecoach driver.

In 1875, he arrived in Wichita, Kansas, where he joined the police force. Wyatt's early career as a policeman in Wichita was a bit undistinguished according to the accounts in the *Wichita Beacon.*

His major arrest in that position took place when he captured a horse thief who had become entangled in a housewife's clothes line. The *Wichita Beacon* found the incident comical, and ran the following tongue-in-cheek account, even misspelling Earp's name. The newspaper's account was run May 12, 1875:

An Aristocratic Horse Thief

On Tuesday evening of last week, the Policeman Erp (sic) in his rounds, ran across a chap whose general appearance and getup answered the description given of one W.W.

12

Compton, who was said to have stolen two horses and a mule from Le Roy (sic), in Coffee county.

Earp took him in tow and required his name which he gave as "Jones". This didn't satisfy the officer who took Mr. Jones into the Gold Room on Douglas Avenue that he might examine him fully by lamplight.

Mr. Jones, not liking the look of things, ran out, running to the rear of Denison's stables. Erp (sic) fired one shot across his poop to bring him to, to use a naughty-cal phrase, and just as he did so, the man cast anchor near a clothesline, hauled down his colors and surrendered without firing a gun.

The officer laid hold of him and before he could recover his feet for another run, and taking him to the jail placed him in the keeping of the sheriff.

On the way to the jail "Jones" acknowledged he was the man wanted; the fact of the arrest was telegraphed to the sheriff of Coffey County who came down Thursday night and removed Compton to the jail of that county.

A black horse and a buggy were found at one of the feed stables where Compton had left them. After stealing the stock at Coffey he went to Independence where he traded them for the buggy, stole the black horse and came to this place.

He will probably have the opportunity to do the state service for some years only to come out and go to horse stealing again, until

*a piece of twisted hemp or a stray bullet puts
an end to his hankering after horse flesh.*

*Wyatt Earp gained a reputation for being fast with a gun while
serving on Dodge City's police force.   (Kansas Historical Society)*

Before Earp could become a seasoned policeman, he assaulted William Smith, a candidate for Wichita city marshal. Wyatt was charged with "violating the peace and order of the city," according to the *Wichita Beacon,* and ordered by Judge Atwood to turn in his badge.

Wyatt's brother Morgan Earp was in town and seeking a place on the Wichita police force at the time of Wyatt's trouble. Both Wyatt and Morgan were ordered to leave town or face arrest as vagrants.

The brothers headed for Dodge City, which had been called "that wicked little city" by the *Washington Star*. Wyatt became a faro dealer at the famous Long Branch Saloon, and was appointed a deputy or assistant policeman there in 1876.

When he was reappointed in 1878, he was praised by the *Dodge City Times* as a competent officer. The *Times* warned would-be bad men, "Do not pull a gun on Earp unless you got the drop and meant to burn powder without any preliminary talk."

Quelling a band of rowdy cowboys was not always an easy job.   (Library of Congress)

Earp was not always the gentleman. When a group of drunken Texas cowhands came into town, Wyatt was assailed by a muscular dance hall girl named "Miss Frankie Bell" when he attempted to quiet the cowboys.

When Miss Frankie Bell cursed Wyatt for curtailing the activities of the rowdy cowboys, Earp slapped her and dragged her to the calaboose for the night, where she was fined $20 for her behavior.

But neither did City fathers like their policemen slapping women. Wyatt was assessed the lowest fine affordable, one dollar.

Always the rover, Earp, in 1879, joined his brothers and their wives in Tombstone, Arizona. His initial plan was to establish a stage line there, but he tossed this plan aside when he learned there were already two such lines in town.

Wyatt lived with his common-law wife Celia (Mattie) Blaylock. Mattie was about twenty-two at the time. Earp later abandoned her. The destitute Mattie worked as a prostitute in the mining town of Pinal, Arizona Territory, to support herself. She died in 1888.

Wyatt met his third wife Josie (Josephine Marcus Earp) in Tombstone, Arizona. She remained with him until his death.

Rustlers, horse thieves, and desperados terrorized Southeastern Arizona. These outlaws were loosely termed the "Cowboy Element". The best known of this "Cowboy Element' was the Clanton Clan, led by N.C. "Old Man" Clanton.

The Clanton family included sons Peter, Joseph Isaac (Ike), Phineas (Phin) and Billy, the youngest and still a teenager. Joining the Clantons in their clandestine operations were the McLaury brothers, Tom and Frank.

Soon after he arrived in Tombstone, Wyatt was appointed deputy sheriff. The job Wyatt really wanted was that of Sheriff.

There was bad blood between the Clantons, and the Earp brothers. Both sides had verbally threatened each other. Virgil Earp, a deputy U.S. Marshall, became embroiled in physical arguments with the McLaurys and Ike Clanton.

Doc Holliday entered the picture at this time. Doc was a dentist by trade, but in the west he was a professional gambler and a close friend of the Earp brothers. Some say it was Doc that was the real source of the trouble between the Earps and the Clanton gang.

During one evening in the Alhambra Saloon, Ike Clanton was drunk and began making threats against the Earps and Doc Holliday. When Doc heard of the threats, he entered the saloon and tried to provoke Clanton into drawing his gun. Ike, however, wasn't armed, as Tombstone had an ordinance against being armed while in town.

Holliday then tried to talk a saloon patron into getting Ike a gun. The argument between Holliday and Clanton was broken up by Morgan Earp, who had been deputized by his brother Virgil, the city marshal. Even so the fight continued into the street.

Ike Clanton then spotted Wyatt Earp, and boasted that he would have him "man for man" the next day. Instead of going to bed, the young Clanton gambled all night, some say in a game that included Sheriff John Behan and City Marshal Virgil Earp.

Clanton was still mouthing threats and carrying a rifle through town the next morning, shouting he would shoot the first Earp that he saw. Virgil Earp, in his position as marshal decided to haul Clanton to court, charging him with violating the town ordinance against carrying firearms.

The court fined Clanton $25 and ordered him to surrender his rifle, leaving him unarmed. The young outlaw continued his threat to get even with the Earps.

Wyatt gave what is now his famous response: "If you are so anxious to make a fight, I will go anywhere on earth to make a fight with you."

On October 26, 1881, the Clantons and McLaurys were at the O.K. Corral. They planned to get their horses and head home, but at the same time, they were still making threats against the Earps.

Word got back to Marshal Virgil Earp, who then decided to deputize Doc Holliday. This meant that every man in the Earp party was now a lawman.

Despite the legend of Wyatt Earp, no shooting actually took place at the O.K. Corral. As the Earps and Doc made their way through town, they passed the O.K. Corral, but the Clantons and McLaurys were not there. They were waiting in the alley by Fly's Photo Shop.

When they were spotted by Virgil, he told them, "Throw up your hands. I have come to disarm you."

According to witnesses, Billy Clanton said, "Don't shoot me. I don't want to fight."

Tom McLaury opened his coat, showing that he too, was unarmed. Ike Clanton ran up to Wyatt, but no one knows for sure who fired first.

Wyatt Earp gave this account:

> *I knew that Frank McLaury had the reputation of being a good shot and a dangerous man, and I aimed at Frank McLaury...My first shot struck Frank McLaury in the belly...If Tom McLaury was unarmed I did not know it.*

Sheriff John Behan, who saw the shootout, gave this version:

> *...the first man that I was certain was hit was Frank McLaury, as I saw him staggering and bewildered and knew he was hit...Ike Clanton broke and ran after the first few shots were fired; Ike, I think, went through Fly's Building; the last I saw of him he was*

18

running through the back of Fly's Building toward Allen Street.

R.J. Coleman, who also witnessed the event, gave this account:

Billy Clanton stood in the same position I first saw him; saw him fire two or three shots in a crouched position; one of them hit Morgan Earp, who stumbled or fell, he jumped up again and commenced shooting...I think Billy Clanton must have been struck, but was down in a crouching position, and using the pistol across his knee and fired two shots, one of which hit Marshal (Virgil) Earp; Wyatt and Morgan were still firing at him, when he raised himself up and then fell, still holding his pistol in his hand.

Billy Clanton, Tom and Frank McLaury soon died. The only armed person without injury was Wyatt Earp. Sheriff Behan arrested Wyatt for murder. Three days after the shoot-out, the coroner held an inquest. The Earps moved into the Cosmopolitan Hotel, which was deemed to be safer for them than their own homes.

Several witnesses, including Sheriff Behan and Ike Clanton testified at the inquest. At the conclusion of the inquest, the ten jurors found:

...After viewing the body and hearing such testimony as had been submitted to us, find that the person was Frank McLaury...and that he came to his death in the town of Tombstone in said county, and on the 26th day of October, 1881, from the effects of pistol and gunshot wounds inflicted by Virgil Earp,

19

Morgan Earp, Wyatt Earp and one Holliday,
commonly called Doc Holliday.
   ...The verdict in the case of William
Clanton and Thomas McLaury was the same
as above.

Wyatt asked that he not be arrested on the day of the shooting so that he could attend to his wounded brothers. On November 4, 1881, Wyatt, along with Doc Holliday, was arrested and charged with the murders of the McLaurys and Billy Clanton.

It was fortunate for Wyatt that his friend, Wells Spicer, was the presiding judge. The judge allowed Wyatt to testify by reading a statement prepared by his lawyer. The defense lawyers had no cross examination.

Among the dozen witnesses was H.F. Sills, a railroad engineer who testified he heard the Clantons and McLaurys say they were going to "kill Virgil Earp."

To Judge Spicer, facts about Ike Clanton were the most important. His taunting threats had started the whole affair, but Clanton was not injured at all. Part of Judge Spicer's opinion, issued December 1, 1881, follows:

   ...the great fact, most prominent in the
matter, to wit, that Isaac Clanton was not
injured at all, and could have been killed
first and easiest...I...cannot resist firm
conviction that the Earps acted wisely,
discreetly, and prudentially to secure their
own self preservation—they saw at once the
dire necessity of giving the first shot to save
themselves from certain death...it was a
necessary act done in the discharge of official
duty.

The story didn't end there. Judge Spicer received a threat that he would be assassinated. (He wasn't.) On December 28, 1881, Virgil Earp, who was still marshal, was shot in the left arm while crossing the street. He was not able to use his left arm again.

The next month, Morgan Earp was playing billiards in a Tombstone saloon when he was shot in the back. He died from the gunshot. Another bullet narrowly missed Wyatt.

Wyatt killed the man who shot his brother.

The famous gunfight at the O.K. Corral was over in twenty or thirty seconds, according to Sheriff Behan. The countless versions depicting the battle in movies, television and radio documentaries were not only exaggerated, but distorted and greatly fictionalized.

Nevertheless, even the acquittal of the Earps and Doc Holliday was the beginning of their end in Tombstone. Virgil Earp was relieved of his marshal's badge. Wyatt was forced to give up his gambling concession at the Oriental Saloon

Wyatt and Josie Earp eventually settled in California where they grew old together. Doc Holliday returned to Colorado where he died of tuberculosis in a sanitarium.

Wyatt Earp spent his final years working mining claims in the Mojave Desert. He and Josie would spend the summer in Los Angeles where they befriended early Hollywood actors. The Earps lived off real estate and mining investments.

Wyatt died in Los Angeles at the age of 80 of chronic cystitis on January 13, 1929. His wife Josie had his ashes buried in her family's plot in Colma, California, near San Francisco. When she died in 1944, her remains, too, were buried next to Wyatt's.

The Fence-Cutting Wars

Ira Aten, Texas Ranger
(Texas Rangers Hall of Fame)

When barbed wire was first introduced on the range people objected to the free range being fenced. Many of them began cutting fences, especially on the large ranches.

Working under cover as a ranch hand, Texas Ranger Ira Aten investigated and helped reduce the fence-cutting. Along some fences that had been cut several times, Aten placed "dynamite bombs".

"I fixed the bombs so that when the fence was cut between the posts it would jerk a small wire laid under the grass to the cap and explode the bombs," he said in his memoir.

Although the Adjutant General did not approve the method and ordered Aten to remove the bombs, he still exploded several more. The word got out that the bombs were planted on all the fences in Navarro County, effectively stopping the fence cutters in that area.

CHAPTER 2

BAT MASTERSON

'He sometimes used his cane as a club'

Bat Masterson
1855 or 1856-1921
(Google Images)

Bat Masterson just naturally gravitated toward action, and often to trouble as well. As a young man, he got his taste of economic shenanigans early in life. When only seventeen, he and his older brother Ed took jobs grading roadbed for the Atchison, Topeka and Santa Fe Railroad.

Their boss vanished without paying the brothers for their labor. Bat caught up with the man and collected the wages at gunpoint.

Bartholomew Masterson was born November 26, 1853. (Other reports list his birth variously as November 24 and the year as either 1855 or 1856.)

As a young man, he adopted the name William Barclay Masterson. His nickname "Bat" is simply an abbreviated name for "Bartholomew".

Young Masterson, in his late teens, became a buffalo hunter, supplying meat for the railroad crews. He was headquartered at Adobe Walls, Texas. As Bat and his friend Billy Dixon prepared to leave Adobe Walls to hunt buffalo, Comanche and Cheyenne Indians appeared on the distant horizon.

The Indian party was led by Comanche war chief Quanah Parker. The Indians continued to attack the sod building where the white trappers were lodged. The warriors continued the assault for several hours but were hampered because their flaming arrows could not penetrate the sod buildings where the white men were.

The Indian warriors withdrew when army soldiers under General Nelson A. Miles left Fort Worth to take up the battle. Final battle causalities were listed as four white men and thirty Indians.

In the winter of 1872, Bat and his brother Jim shot and butchered up to 20 buffalo each day.

Masterson's first gun fight was in Sweetwater, Texas in 1876 over a girl named Molly Brennan. Melvin A. King, the jilted lover of Molly, attacked Bat when Molly showed an interest in him. During the melee, Bat and Molly were both wounded. Bat shot and killed King. Bat, himself, however, was shot in the pelvis by King and had to carry a cane the rest of his life.

One colorful story is that Masterson got his nickname because he sometimes used his cane as a club during fights. Bat eventually joined his brothers in Dodge City, Kansas. His brother Ed was a deputy sheriff there, while his younger brother Jim was a partner in a saloon.

At the age of twenty-two, Masterson became sheriff of Ford County. Bat was voted out of office in 1879, and he turned to gambling to make a living.

He returned to Denver and began drinking heavily. His reputation as a gunfighter caused the local sheriff to give him an ultimatum. His choices were:

1. Surrender his sidearm; Or
2. Leave town by morning.

Masterson decided to leave town.

He was offered the appointment of marshal to the Oklahoma Territory. Masterson figured that some fame-seeker wanting to make a reputation for himself would confront him and he would have to kill or be killed. This, he said, didn't make any sense in inviting such a thing to happen.

Bat once witnessed a town's marshal being abusive to a man he was attempting to arrest, and Masterson objected to the treatment. Bat was jailed and fined by the marshal, but his fine was later returned by the city council.

Masterson once went to Dodge City and served alongside Wyatt Earp as a sheriff's deputy. There he purchased an interest in the Lone Star dance hall, thinking this would show residents his interest in the town and further his efforts to become county sheriff. He was soon elected County Sheriff of Ford County, Kansas.

His first job as sheriff was chasing the Rourke-Rudabaugh gang who had robbed a train at Kinsley, Kansas. Bat captured all four outlaws, one of which was Dave Rudabaugh, who later rode with Billy the Kid.

Bat lost his bid for re-election when a newspaper editor editorialized that Masterson was exorbitant in his spending while bringing seven Cheyenne prisoners to trial. Bat's popularity suffered also for his association with the "Gang", a group of town administrators led by Mayor James H. (Dog) Kelley, who were opposed to the reform element.

After losing his sheriff's job, Bat made a living at cards and faro. In February 1881, he accompanied Wyatt Earp and Luke Short to Tombstone, where he worked as a dealer at the Oriental Saloon.

Despite his meanderings, Masterson considered Denver, Colorado, his hometown. He bought the Palace Variety Theater, where he met and married Emma Walters, a singer and dancer, in 1889, although their union was not officially legalized until about 1891. No children were born to the couple.

Bat spent most of his time in the gambling house, but also took an avid interest in the boxing game, which during the 1880s was promoted and controlled by professional gamblers. Masterson attended almost every important fisticuff event in the country over the next 40 years.

He became a ring official, a promoter and a boxing columnist. The National Police Gazette hailed Masterson in 1893 as the "King of Western Sporting Men". He promoted prizefighters John L. Sullivan and Jim Corbett. He also wrote a weekly sports column for a Denver newspaper.

In 1896, a prize fight between Bob Fitzsimmons and Peter Maher to determine the new heavyweight champion was set to be held in El Paso.

When promoters, gamblers, dance hall girls and the fighters themselves flocked to the area to ready for the fight, the Texas governor was outraged. There was a state law prohibiting prize fights, and the governor sent in the Texas Rangers to stop this one. Bat arrived in town to make sure the fight went on. He escorted Tom O'Rourke, who held the ten thousand dollar purse.

Because of the pressure from the governor's office, promoter Dan Stuart moved the event from Denver to Langtry, Texas where Judge Roy Bean ruled. A ring was built a few hundred yards away in Mexican Territory.

The fight was almost a farce. In less than two minutes, Fitzsimmons decked Maher for the count. Masterson made sure that Fitzsimmons got his prize money. He then returned to Denver and wrote about the fight in his weekly column.

Bat became embroiled in a fight with rival club owner Otto Flotto, who had a grudge against Bat for a reason Masterson didn't understand. The two fought it out in the street one day, with Bat getting the upper hand.

Masterson later sold out his club interest, said farewell to Denver, and headed to New York.

He arrived there while Teddy Roosevelt was president. Roosevelt appointed Bat as U.S. deputy marshal of New York. Bat also worked as an editor for the New York Morning Telegraph, where he turned out a popular sports column three times a week.

When Roosevelt left office, Bat was fired from his marshal's job, but continued writing his sports columns.

Masterson was arrested on a street corner in New York by two detectives who booked him on charges of running a crooked faro game. They relieved him of his large pistol.

The arrest story filled the front pages of the city's newspapers. New Yorkers were fascinated by a real-life western man-killer, toting a six-shooter with which he had dispatched two dozen or more bad men.

Bat's arrest was the result of a complaint filed by George H. Snow, a Mormon elder who claimed he had been swindled out of $16,000 in a braced faro game. Bat was arraigned and released on twenty-five-hundred dollars bond pending a hearing the following Monday.

Snow failed to appear at the hearing and the judge dismissed the swindling charge against Masterson, but fined him ten dollars for carrying a concealed weapon.

On October 25, 1921, Masterson went to work as usual. In the middle of typing his sports column, he was seized with a heart attack. He died at his sports desk. His wife died in 1932.

CHAPTER 3

PAT GARRETT

'The unluckiest lawman of them all'

Pat Garrett, at nineteen years of age, left a prosperous plantation in Louisiana in 1869 to go to Dallas County, Texas. There, he worked as a cowboy until 1875. He then tried buffalo hunting.

Garrett and another hunter disagreed over some buffalo hides. The other man drew on Garrett, who still beat him to the draw and shot him dead.

In 1879, Garrett married Juanita Gutierrez, who died before the end of the year. He then married her sister, Apolinaria.

Pat Garrett
1850-1908
(Google Images

Garrett was appointed Lincoln County sheriff in 1880, when the Lincoln County War was drawing to a close. The Lincoln County conflict was a turf battle between two entrenched business operators over who would supply beef to the government to feed the Indians on the reservations.

29

John Tunstall did not feel that one outfit should control so much power as did the present supplier of beef. So he bought a sizeable ranch in the county, and defiantly challenged the beef monopoly by building a big general store.

He made his prices competitive and won many of the rancher accounts over from Dolan and Riley, who had had the beef business cornered for years. This infuriated the powerful pair. Dolan and Riley issued immediate threats of arson and even death if Tunstall didn't desist.

These threats forced Tunstall and his partners to hire bodyguards for protection. It was into this fray that walked Billy the Kid.

In 1877, William Bonney, known as Billy the Kid, a gun-proud youngster, entered the services of John Tunstall. Billy worshiped Tunstall. He said, "He was the only man who ever treated me kindly, like I was free born and white."

Billy proved loyal and showed Tunstall he also had savvy. While his small, wiry frame and boyish smile did not fit the standard of a bodyguard, his lightning quick draw and willingness to challenge enemies made up for it.

"That's the finest lad I ever met," Tunstall told his partner John Chisum. "He's a revelation to me every day and would do anything to please me. He has his immature ways, but bless me, I'm going to make a man out of that boy some day. You wait and see."

Riley and Dolan then trumped up a number of charges against Tunstall, among them the claim that he had stolen some cattle. A paid-off judge, who heard the charges, upheld them. When Sheriff William Brady and his posse attempted to confiscate part of Tunstall's cattle herd to pay the judgment, Tunstall was killed.

Tunstall's murder was a real turning point in Billy's life. He flipped crazily with anger. Billy thus became deeply embroiled in The Lincoln County War. He joined a group called the Regulators and ended up killing Sheriff William Brady along with other men involved in the fighting.

When Pat Garrett took the sheriff's position, Garrett's first goal was to take care of Billy the Kid. By the end of the year, he had captured Billy the Kid and killed two of his cronies, including Tom O'Folliard. The *New Mexican* newspaper called Garrett the "hero of the hour."

Garrett took Billy the Kid to Mesilla, New Mexico for trial. A jury convicted him and he was sentenced to hang at Lincoln, the county seat. He was hardly ensconced in the county jail before he escaped.

Garrett then followed Billy to the Pete Maxwell house, some seventy five miles north of Roswell, New Mexico. About midnight, Garrett hid in a darkened bedroom and waited for Billy.

Billy entered the room and saw Garrett's shadow. "Quien es?" (Who is it?) he asked in Spanish, while drawing his gun. Without speaking, Garrett shot him square in the heart.

Ironically, Garrett became more of a villain than he did a hero. He had killed a favorite son of the populace who could not get enough of the escapades of "Billy the Kid". Garrett then lost his re-election attempt for sheriff of Lincoln County.

It would seem Garrett's luck could not get any worse, but worse it became. For one thing, he never received the $500 reward money for the capture or killing of "Billy the Kid".

Garrett next moved from Lincoln County to Tascosa in the Texas Panhandle. There, he served as captain of a group of Texas Rangers assigned by Texas Governor John Ireland to protect ranchers from cattle rustlers. The job soon dissatisfied him and within weeks he quit the Rangers and returned to New Mexico, going this time to Roswell.

Here, he devised a scheme to irrigate the desert. His bad luck held, as the area had both impoverished soil and bad water. Garrett then ran for sheriff of Chavez County, which had been carved out of Lincoln County. He lost.

A murder took place in southeastern New Mexico that proved a turning point in Garrett's life. The shooting to death of Colonel Albert Jennings Fountain and his eight year-old son Henry on a lonely stretch of desert brought about a storm of lawlessness similar to the Lincoln County War.

The feud was between Fountain, a Republican who was a member of the Southeastern New Mexico Stock Growers Association, and Albert Fall, a Democrat who openly associated with cattle thieves.

Fountain had secured indictments against rustlers and against a powerful New Mexico rancher named Oliver Lee. Fall was a self-taught lawyer that opposed Fountain's pursuit of the thieves. Some evidence linked Fall and Lee to the murder of Fountain and his son.

New Mexico Governor William T. Thornton remembered Pat Garrett and his successful pursuit of Billy the Kid. He brought Garrett back from Uvalde, Texas, to New Mexico. He then helped get Pat installed as sheriff in Las Cruces, the seat of Dona Ana County where the Fountain murders occurred.

Garrett worked his way through a minefield of potentially violent encounters. He finally arrested Oliver Lee and a ranch hand and charged them with the murder of Colonel Fountain and his son Henry. Represented in court by attorney Albert Fall, the two men won acquittal, bringing another loss to the unlucky Pat Garrett.

Things improved when Garrett was reelected sheriff in Las Cruces for two more terms. Another upbeat happened in his life when President Theodore Roosevelt appointed Garrett as El Paso Collector of Customs on December 20,

1901. This required Garrett to move forty miles south to the border city.

Garrett undid his good luck streak by forming a friendship with Tom Powers, a one-eyed El Paso gambler and saloonkeeper. Powers was run out of Wisconsin for beating his own father into a coma. Garrett refused to heed the caution of friends about his association with Powers.

One time, he even took Powers with him to attend a reunion of President Roosevelt's old combat unit, the Rough Riders, in San Antonio. This was an embarrassment to Roosevelt, and when Garrett's term as Collector of Customs expired, Roosevelt did not reappoint him.

Garrett, discouraged and broke, his reputation stained by his killing of Billy the Kid, was despondent over the downtrends in his life.

He was hard-pressed to pay his creditors and eventually put his ranch up for sale.

While riding in a buggy with Carl Adamson, a prospective buyer of the ranch, they met Wayne Brazel, a cowboy who was leasing Garrett's ranch. Garrett was angry with Brazel for placing eighteen hundred goats on the property and had tried to break the lease.

Brazel was adamant. The only way he would cancel the lease was if the prospective ranch buyers would purchase the goats. This stipulation was stifling the sale of the property, as the prospective buyers had no use for eighteen hundred goats.

Garrett was infuriated. He told Brazel he would get him and his goats off the property one way or another. Adamson stepped out of the wagon to urinate and Garrett decided to do the same.

Both men had their backs to Brazel. A shot rang out and Garrett crashed to the ground. The bullet from behind shattered his skull. A second bullet struck him in the stomach while he lay on the ground.

The fifty-seven-year-old Garrett never uttered a word before dying. Brazel surrendered his revolver to Adamson and the two men rode into Las Cruces where Brazel surrendered to authorities.

Garrett's body had been left where it fell until found by a sheriff's posse. The fly of his pants was unbuttoned and his lower pants leg was still damp from urine spray. A wet puddle of sand was at his feet. His left hand was ungloved, while his shooting hand contained a glove.

His shotgun was found at the scene, located about three feet from his body. The undisturbed nature of the sand around the shotgun would indicate that the weapon was placed where it was found and not thrown down in a death jerk reaction.

Investigator Captain Fred Fornoff, New Mexico Mounted Police, called Brazel's self-defense plea into question. At the site, he found unexplained hoof prints, horse dung and an empty Winchester rifle shell casing. An unknown assassin? Someone in addition to Brazel?

Within a few weeks, a grand jury indicted Brazel on a charge of first degree murder. The trial lasted one day. The jury acquitted Wayne Brazel. No one considered Fornoff's evidence.

Garrett had tried all his life to be a good lawman, even though he failed in the eyes of the public. In death, he suffered the ultimate indignity by getting shot in the back while taking a piss!

The Battle of San Jacinto

The Battle of San Jacinto was the turning point in a series of events that would affect the geographic sovereignty of North America. On a monument near Houston, these words best describe the War:

Measured by its results, San Jacinto was one of the decisive battles of the world. The freedom of Texas from Mexico won here led to annexation and the Mexican War, resulting in the acquisition by the United States of the Texas, New Mexico, Arizona, Nevada, California, Utah, and parts of Colorado, Wyoming, Kansas and Oklahoma.

First U.S. Train Robbery

Frank Reno
(NineMSN)

The Reno Brothers committed what is believed to be the first train robbery in the United States. This crime has been incorrectly attributed to the James Gang, headed by Jesse James.

The train robbers boarded the Ohio and Mississippi train as it pulled out of the Seymour, Indiana depot. A guard was knocked unconscious, and two safes were pushed out the door of the moving car.

One safe, containing fifteen-thousand-dollars was broken open. The second safe, containing thirty-thousand-dollars was not broken.

CHAPTER 4

BILL TILGHMAN

'The greatest sheriff of the Wild West period'

Billy Tilghman was scarcely seventeen years old when he turned to buffalo hunting on the edge of Indian Territory in Kansas. While Indians were not allowed outside their reservation under treaty restrictions, they seldom observed the rules.

Bill Tilghman
1854-1924
(Google Images)

Tilghman and his partners returned to their camp after a day's hunt to find it a complete wreck. Indians had raided the camp, destroying several hundred dollars worth of buffalo hides and stealing all the foodstuff they could find.

The young buffalo hunters now had to decide what to do with the twenty-five hides they had harvested that day. Tilghman's partners were for moving away the first thing in the morning for fear the Indians would return.

"We're liable to all be killed if we stay here any longer," said one of them.

Billy, however, had a different strategy. He directed one partner to hitch up the team and drive to Griffin's Ranch and get a sack of flour, some coffee and sugar, and a sack of grain for the horses.

Griffin's Ranch was fifteen miles north on the Medicine Lodge River, the only place with supplies nearer than Wichita.

Meanwhile, Tilghman and the other partner staked out the twenty five buffalo hides harvested the day before so they would dry. If the Cheyennes came again, Billy said, he would be ready them.

"I don't intend to stop shooting as long as there is one of them in sight," he vowed.

For several years, Tilghman, with his brothers and friends from Atchison County, formed partnerships in the shooting, skinning and selling of buffalo robes and meat. Tilghman became well-known to the Cheyennes and Osages and spent many days in their camps.

Bill was forced to show his marksmanship ability to the Indians when one of his close friends, "Hurricane Bill" Martin, boasted to an Indian chief about Tilghman's sharp shooting. Roman Nose, the Cheyenne chief, demanded proof of his skill with a rifle.

Bill brought his Sharps rifle to the Cheyenne camp. Roman Nose examined the rifle, then pointed to two buffalo bulls grazing on a small rise far from camp. Using a rifle rest, Tilghman took aim and fired. Twice his shots fell short, but on the third shot, the Indians grunted when a bull buffalo toppled over.

"Hurricane Bill" Martin insisted that the distance be measured. The Indians and the white men agreed that the distance was one full mile. It is said that of the eleven thousand buffalo killed that winter, Tilghman's Sharps rifle accounted for seventy-five hundred of them.

Tilghman carried this steadfastness into his job as a deputy sheriff in Ford County, Kansas in 1877. He was known for his unwavering courage more than for being a fast draw and a keen marksman with a gun.

Bill Doolin
(Google Images)

His most celebrated arrest was that of William "Bill" Doolin, a notorious member of the Dalton Gang, who carried a five thousand dollar reward on his head. Tilghman tracked the outlaw to a bathhouse in Eureka Springs, Arkansas, where he not only captured

Bill Doolin
(Google Images)

him alive, but transported him to the Guthrie, Oklahoma jail without the aid of handcuffs or restraints.

Tilghman noticed a small silver mug in the room where he arrested Doolin. The outlaw told him it was a present for his infant son. Tilghman made sure the son got the mug.

Doolin escaped from the Guthrie County jail and went on the outlaw trail again. He was later shot to death by a U.S. marshal.

As a deputy sheriff, Tilghman would earn the moniker of "the man who drove the outlaws out of Oklahoma." Tilghman learned early on that to be a successful sheriff it was just as necessary to be a good politician. Tilghman cultivated the press as evidenced in this 1907 story in the *Lincoln Broadsides* published in Lincoln County, Oklahoma.

39

I desire to call to the attention of the voters to the good work done by Wm. Tilghman during his tenure as Lincoln County Sheriff. During the first 30 days of Mr. Tilghman's administration, he received warrants for nine persons charged with horse stealing. He caught eight of the thieves, recovered the horse in the ninth case and afterwards caught the thief and sent him to the penitentiary, a record for thirty days never made by any sheriff before or since that time.

During the 10 years prior to his election there have been convicted and sentenced to the penitentiary 39 persons charged with various crimes. During his term in office 84 persons were convicted and sentenced to the penitentiary, being more than has ever been sent to the penitentiary before or since his terms as sheriff. A large portion of these were the hardest criminals Lincoln County ever had to deal with, a good many of them being horse thieves, bank robbers, and murderers...

This record was accomplished by hard work...(He) kept going until he captured them and landed them in jail and kept them until they were indicted and convicted. He then transported them to the penitentiary...

Mr. Tilghman inaugurated a system of collecting personal taxes that saved the farmers of Lincoln County hundreds of dollars...Do you want Lincoln County overrun with horse thieves? Do you want to guard your pastures to protect your stock at night? Do you want Lincoln County to continue to be a banner county in Oklahoma for bank robbers? Do you want Lincoln County

40

murderers to escape and go unpunished? Do you want your homes burglarized? If not, vote for Wm. Tilghman on June 8th.

Some historians claim Bill Tilghman was the greatest sheriff of the Wild West period. He arrested more men, shattered more outlaw gangs, and jailed more criminals than any other peace officer of the era.

Tilghman's formal education was scant. He left home at age fifteen and spent most of his next fifteen years living with the Indians. Over a five year period as a buffalo hunter, he killed an estimated 12,000 of the animals, which caused some conflict with local Native Americans. In a skirmish with the Cheyenne Indians, Tilghman killed seven Indian braves.

Two years later, Tilghman narrowly escaped being lynched after he was falsely accused of murdering a man in Granada, Colorado.

Even though he was a life-long teetotaler, Tilghman opened a saloon in Dodge City in 1875. Three years later, he accepted the offer of his friend, Bat Masterson, to become his deputy sheriff. He developed a reputation for being both courageous and honest. He later became marshal of Dodge City.

When Oklahoma was opened to settlement on the historic day of April 22, 1889, Tilghman was one of the first arrivals and established his home at Guthrie. Tilghman rarely resorted to violence in his law duties. During his long career as a lawmen, he is said to have killed only two criminals in gun fights.

Tilghman, Heck Thomas and Chris Madsen became known as the Three Guardsmen and were credited with wiping out organized crime in Oklahoma. This included the hunting down of Bill Doolin and his gang.

Some say Tilghman was paid more reward money than any other law officer.

In 1891, he was appointed a deputy United States marshal. He was reappointed by every succeeding U.S. marshal for the next nineteen years.

During his career, Tilghman was a frontier scout, buffalo hunter, peace officer, movie maker, and state senator. He missed being a lawman, and resigned from the state senate to take the job of chief of police in Oklahoma City.

In 1924, at age seventy-two, Tilghman was shot and killed by a drunken off-duty federal Prohibition Agent named Wiley Lynn. Tilghman had arrested Lynn and disarmed him of his service revolver.

He was unaware that the agent had another pistol secreted on his person. Lynn used that weapon to kill Tilghman.

Ironically, Tilghman's killer was found not guilty because the jury felt his extreme drunkenness exonerated him from the crime. After his acquittal, the agent returned to duty as a federal law enforcement agent.

John "Liver-Eating" Johnson

John Johnson
(Google Images)

John Johnson was a mountain man who trapped deer, bear and hunted buffalo in 1870. He had a cabin on Rock Creek, near Red Lodge, Montana.

He had his own private war with the Crow Indians who had murdered his Indian wife and child. Johnson killed dozens of the tribe members over the next decade.

One easterner who hired Johnson to take him on a trip to hunt bear, said he witnessed Johnson killing two Indians and wounding several others. He casually butchered the two corpses and ate their livers.

Johnson, in 1880, was appointed sheriff of Coulson, Montana. He always settled disputes with his fists and boasted that he never had to shoot a man to keep peace. He carried a rifle around town, but never a six-gun.

CHAPTER 5

HENRY PLUMMER

'He was unable to stay out of trouble'

Henry Plummer worked both sides of the law. He was a sheriff in Montana, and was hung by vigilantes on the very gallows that he had built while a sheriff to hang criminals.

His venture into western lore begins when he was nineteen years old. In April, 1852, Henry sailed from New York to Panama on a mail ship. He traveled by mule train to Panama City, then boarded another ship for the journey to California.

Plummer arrived in San Francisco twenty-four days later. Soon after arrival, he took a job in a bakery, where he earned enough money to move on to the mining camps in Nevada County.

Henry Plummer
1832-1864
(Google Images)

Documents show he acquired a ranch outside Nevada City, California. At some point, he traded some of his mining shares for the Empire Bakery in Nevada City. By 1856, local residents were impressed with Plummer and persuaded him to run for sheriff.

At age 24, Henry Plummer became marshal of Nevada City, the largest settlement in California. He won re-election a year later, in 1857, but then his troubles began.

Henry was accused of having an affair with the wife of a miner named John Vedder. When the angry husband confronted him, the two competed in a duel which Henry easily won. Soon after, he was arrested and tried for murder in a sensational and emotionally charged trial that went twice to the California Supreme Court, where he was eventually convicted and sentenced to ten years in San Quentin Prison.

Local residents quickly petitioned the Governor for a pardon for the ex-sheriff, maintaining that Henry had acted in self-defense. Plummer convinced the court that he suffered from tuberculosis and was granted an early release for health reasons after serving six months of his sentence.

Plummer then returned to Nevada City and became a regular customer at the many brothels operating day and night. He was soon penniless and resorted to joining a band of road agents that robbed stagecoaches. In one robbery, the stagecoach driver escaped with both his passengers and his cargo, but Plummer was caught and arrested. He stood trial but was acquitted due to lack of evidence.

Henry was simply unable to stay out of trouble. Next he got into a brawl with a man over a dance hall girl. He shot and killed the man and was rearrested. He escaped what was a sure stay in prison by bribing a jailor before he could be tried. Plummer fled to Oregon.

Somewhere along the way, Henry met Jim Mayfield, also wanted by the law. Plummer then devised a clever, even ingenious, scheme. He would play dead. He sent word to California newspapers that both he and Mayfield had been hanged in Washington. He forged the signature of a local sheriff. The ruse had the desired effect, and the pair no longer had to look back over their shoulders for a pursuing posse.

Wherever he went, trouble seemed to follow. He arrived in Lewiston, Idaho with a woman companion, registering at the Luna House. Working in a casino, Henry soon ran across Cyrus Skinner, an old cellmate from his incarceration at San Quentin. Along with Skinner were a number of other "wanted" men, including Club Foot George Lane and Bill Bunton.

They formed a gang and began preying on local families in the gold camps, and hitting hard on the gold shipments leaving the mines. Plummer abandoned his mistress, a woman with three children, who then resorted to prostitution to feed herself and family.

Henry concentrated on the area between Elk City, Florence and Lewiston, Idaho. In Orofino, Idaho, a saloon keeper named Patrick Ford booted Plummer and his companions out of his saloon. After they left, Ford followed them to the livery stable where he fired on them. Henry returned the fire and killed Ford.

The saloon keepers friends began gathering a lynch mob. Plummer hightailed it out of town, headed east to Montana. In Montana, Plummer killed a man by the name of Jack Cleveland. It is believed the reason for the killing was that Cleveland threatened to expose Plummer's past.

In May 1863, Henry was supposedly on the good side of the law. He was elected sheriff of Bannack, Montana. Bannack was the wildest, woolliest town in the whole Idaho Territory. Holdups occurred daily and killings were just as frequent. The outlaws took what they wanted and killed all the witnesses.

Unknown to the people of Bannack, Henry, their newly-elected sheriff, was actually the leader of a 100-man gang involved in local robberies. Because of the great number in the gang, the members wore ties in a special knot to identify themselves as fellow members.

The gang called themselves the "Innocents". Crime in the town increased dramatically with the election of Plummer to the sheriff's post. More than 100 citizens were murdered soon after he took office.

A vigilante committee was formed, and it was then that a member of the "Innocents" confessed that Plummer was actually the leader of the gang. The vigilantes didn't waste time with a trial.

Seven months after the "Innocents" began their reign of terror, Henry Plummer was marched to the scaffold that he himself had built in his role as sheriff. Moments before the vigilantes could hang him, Plummer made an unusual request.

"Give me two hours and a good horse, and I'll bring back my weight in gold."

The vigilantes answered his request by quickly stringing him up from the scaffold he had ordered built. Henry Plummer was lynched by the vigilantes on January10, 1864.

Immediately after his hanging, gold hunters began looking for Plummer's buried treasure. In the early 1900's, two mysterious men rode into Bannack with a very dirty long-box they wanted to secure in a vault overnight.

The only place with a vault was the bank, and one man stayed at the bank riding shotgun all night. The next morning, they disappeared.

Henry Plummer
Finally Gets a Trial

One hundred twenty nine years after he was hanged without a trial, Henry Plummer's case finally went before a jury. A group of scholars from Twin Bridges, Montana questioned the action of the vigilantes that hung Plummer, and questioned whether he was actually guilty or not.

The case became assignments in the classroom of instructor Mark Weber. He assigned term papers to two students. One used Dimsdale's "The Vigilantes of Montana" while another researched the opposing view, using Mather and Boswell's book, "Hanging the Sheriff".

The two reports portrayed dissimilar versions of Plummer, and students began questioning which version was correct. The idea for a trial was born.

Judge Barbara Brook was asked to preside over the belated trial. Adult jury members were selected and attorney Doug Smith advised the students on jurisprudence.

Students were assigned to play prosecuting and defending attorneys for the Plummer trial. Students also dressed in period costume to play the historical characters that would most likely have been called to testify if Plummer had indeed had a trial.

After all the known elements were laid out and both the defense and prosecutors had made their case, Judge Brook sent the jurors to the jury room. The courtroom was crowded with spectators who wanted to hear the verdict.

When the jury returned, Judge Brook read the verdict. "Please stand Sheriff Plummer and face the jury. We the jury, duly impaneled and sworn to try the issues in the above-entitled action, unanimously find the defendant..."

and Judge Brook halted. "Sheriff Plummer, the jury is unable to render a unanimous decision as required by law. You are free to go."

The packed courtroom and jury applauded the efforts of the young and gifted students. They had done their job well. Jury foreman, Pat Bradley, a judge herself, said that the jury took their job very seriously. "If they had been in the room (jury room) for two weeks they would not have been able to come up with an unanimous decision."

Results of the student trial were carried in 72 newspapers, historical journals, on radio and television in ten western states.

Two months after the trial, Montana's pardon board received what Executive Secretary Craig Thomas described as "an unusual request". It was an application to be pardoned submitted by a man who had been dead for 129 years. It was signed by R.E. Mather, one of the authors of "Hanging the Sheriff", and dated 1 July 1993.

Two other letters were submitted by Frederick Morgan, a publisher of Western history books, and by Jack Burrows, an author and western history professor.

Montana Governor Marc Racicot assured petitioners that the pardon would receive prompt attention by the Board of Pardons.

In August, 1993, the Board of Pardons responded, saying that since Henry Plummer was never convicted by a court, the panel could not review a request for clemency.

At least Plummer finally had his day in court.

The Shootout at Gold Flat

Outlaw bandit Jim Webster used Gold Flat, near Nevada City, California, as his headquarters. Webster had a price on his head but occasionally became bold enough to venture into town.

At the time, Gold City was a bustling little village. It had two stores, a butcher shop, four boarding houses, six saloons and the Round Tent gambling house.

In the jail break of 1856, only one store remained. It was evident to the remaining residents that something was amiss when two unattended horses were spotted in Gold Flat.

Sheriff W.W. Wright and his deputy were riding to Gold City toward the spot where the horses had been seen. In the meantime, Gold Flat resident William Wallace gathered his neighbors and hid near the horses, awaiting the return of the outlaws and the possibility of reward money.

As it became dark, the Gold Flat men in hiding heard men approaching and readied their weapons.

Shots were fired and returned.

When light was brought to the shootout, the men in hiding found they had just shot their sheriff and his deputy. The lawmen died the next day.

CHAPTER 6

ELFEGO BACA

'He appointed himself to be sheriff'

Elfego Baca
1865-1945
(Rio Grande Historical Collections)

One story says that Elfego Baca was born in the middle of a baseball game. His mother, who was nine months pregnant, was one of the players.

Elfego's entry into law enforcement was almost as dramatic. Silver was discovered in the Magdalena Mountains west of Socorro in 1867. Socorro was the largest city in New Mexico, where law and order was virtually non-existent.

Baca wanted to be a lawman. Socorro County didn't have a sheriff, so the nineteen-year-old Elfego appointed himself to the position. Armed with a mail order badge and two pistols, Baca appointed two deputies and then sought indictments against all known criminals in the county.

He devised a unique system for making arrests. He sent a letter to each of the accused, claiming, "I have a warrant here for your arrest. Please come in by (Date)

53

and give yourself up. If you don't, I'll know you intend to resist arrest, and I will feel justified in shooting you on sight when I come after you."

The method proved extremely effective. Many of the wanted men came into town, turned in their guns, and stood trial.

A town known as Frisco (Now called Reserve) was about 120 miles south of Socorro. Here, cowboys came into town to do some serious drinking and hell-raising. One group of cowboys from the Slaughter Ranch liked to have some fun at the expense of some of the Mexicans who lived in Frisco.

These cowboys did cruel things to two Mexicans, a man known as El Burro and his friend, Epitacio Martinez. The cowboys "altered" Burro in front of an aghast crowd. When his friend stood up to defend him, the drunken cowboys tied him to a post and used him for target practice.

Frisco Deputy Sheriff Pedro Sarracino was outnumbered and admittedly couldn't handle the raucous cowboys. He rode to Socorro to seek help from Elfego Baca. The men rode back to Frisco and sought warrants from a local Justice of the Peace for the cowboys' arrest.

Because the cowboys numbered more than 150 men, the Justice of the Peace turned them down. Baca was not one to be detoured by minor legalities. He promptly arrested a cowboy named Charlie McCarthy, who had just shot Baca's hat off.

When the rest of the drunken cowboys demanded their friend be released, Baca shot into the crowd, hitting one of them. Another man died when his horse fell on top of him. The cowboys dispersed, but showed up again 80 strong the following day, intent on freeing the incarcerated cowboy, or as an alternative, killing Elfego Baca.

Baca refused the cowboys' demands and a gunfight began. Baca dragged his prisoner to the house of

Geronimo Armijo and barricaded himself inside. The house had thick log walls and a sunken dirt floor, providing protections from the flying bullets.

The cowboys tried to set fire to the roof, but it was covered with sod and wouldn't burn. They attempted to dynamite the building on one corner but failed.

For 33 hours the battle, which came to be known as "The Battle of Frisco", raged. When it ended, Elfego had killed four cowboys and wounded eight others.

Baca eventually agreed to give himself up to Socorro County sheriff Frank Rose, but refused to turn over his guns. He was tried for murder but acquitted after the door of Armijo's house was entered into evidence. It was riddled with more than 400 bullet holes.

Baca's legendary fame took on some of the aspects of Billy the Kid, except Baca was on the side of the law. He was a marshal, a sheriff, a district attorney, school superintendent, and mayor. Elfego's goal was to be a good police officer. He said, "I want the outlaws to hear my steps a block away."

Baca played heavily on his reputation to intimidate outlaws.

In 1888, he became a U.S. Marshal. He served two years. He then began reading law. In December 1894, he was admitted to the bar and joined a Socorro law firm. He practiced law in El Paso on San Antonio Street from 1902 to 1904.

Baca often defended the underdog. One such incident occurred when two ranchers posted a two thousand dollar bond for an elderly sheepherder in Roswell, New Mexico. The man had gotten into trouble with the law and was suppose to appear in court, but when the court date arrived he couldn't be found. The ranchers worried about losing their bond money. Baca offered to help.

Elfego looked around town until he found an elderly Mexican who did not speak English. Baca brought the man before a judge and paid him $25 to declare himself guilty and not say another word. The judge fined him $50 to which he replied, "Gracias."

The judge said, "I'm going to make you Mexicans obey the law in this country, and the next time I find you in my court, I am going to send you to the penitentiary. Do you understand?"

Baca translated, saying, "The judge says that any time you are not treated properly by the people of Roswell, you have to let him know." The man again replied, "Gracias."

The judge did not speak Spanish and became irritated at the conversation in a language he didn't understand. He said he did not like the man's looks and said he was probably an escaped fugitive.

Baca translated the judge's comments, thusly, "The judge says that he is very much impressed with your appearance. He also likes your courtroom manner. He sends his compliments to your mother."

Again, the Mexican replied, "Gracias."

The ranchers angrily told Baca that the man in court was not the one for whom they had posted bond. Baca responded, "What the hell do you care, the case is settled isn't it."

In 1936, Elfego was interviewed by Janet Smith as part of the WPA Federal Writers' Project Collection. In that interview, Elfego said, "I never wanted to kill anybody, but if a man had it in his mind to kill me, I made it my business to get him first."

Elfego Baca was born February 10, 1865. He died August 27, 1945.

Old West Marshal Badges

Virgil Earp wore a badge similar to this in Tombstone.

This badge was worn by Wyatt Earp.

Badge worn in Oklahoma Territory at turn of century.

James Arness wore this type of badge in T.V. series Gunsmoke.

(Badge photos from Google Images.)

CHAPTER 7

BASS REEVES

'A former slave, he couldn't read nor write'

Born a slave in July 1838, Bass Reeves was the first black ever commissioned as a United States deputy marshal west of the Mississippi.

Bass was owned by Colonel George Reeves, who had a total of seven slaves. During his lifetime, Colonel Reeves was a former sheriff of Grayson County, Texas. He was also a tax collector, state legislator and a colonel in the Confederate Army.

Bass Reeves
1838-1910
(Google Images)

As Bass Reeves became older, the Colonel made him a companion and body servant. George Reeves liked Bass. The youth was big and strong, had a quick mind, good manners, and good humor.

The Colonel noted that Bass had the uncanny ability to accurately evaluate people, something which would serve him well later in life. The opening of the Civil War brought a change to Bass Reeves' life.

There are a couple of versions of why Bass parted company with his owner, Colonel Reeves. One version is that there was a furious argument over a card game the two were playing and Bass beat his boss, laying him out cold with his fists.

Because attacking one's master was punishable by death, Bass made a run for Indian Territory. The echoes of "run away nigger" hounded Bass until the Emancipation.

While records of slaves are scanty, it is believed Bass lived with the Seminoles and the Creek Indians, eventually becoming a close friend of the Creek Chief Opothleyaholo. He became fluent in the Creek language and could converse well in the languages of the other Five Civilized Tribes living in Indian Territory.

Young Bass Reeves had an intense interest in firearms. He became well-known for his speed with a pistol. He could draw and shoot with great accuracy from the hip, but his preferred method was to plant himself, then draw "a bead as fine as a spider's web on a frosty morning."

Some described his accuracy as being so fine that "he could shoot the left leg off a contented fly sitting on a mule's ear at a hundred yards and never ruffle a hair."

After the Civil War ended, Bass married a girl named Jennie, who was also from Texas. The couple settled down on a farm near Van Buren, Arkansas, where they raised ten children, five boys and five girls. After Jennie's death, he remarried and began a second family.

Bass Reeves became a Deputy United States Marshal under Judge Isaac Parker, the "Hanging Judge" of Fort Smith. Bass was a big man, towering to more than six feet and weighing one hundred eighty pounds.

The strength of the man was legendary. Once, while riding in the southern regions of the Chickasaw Nation, he came across a group of cowboys attempting to rescue a full-grown steer from a bog along Mud Creek.

The cowboys had roped the steer and were trying to drag it to solid ground. Reeves saw the broken ropes dangling from the neck of the mired creature. Reeves dismounted, stripped off his clothes, and stepped into the bog.

He worked his way to the trapped animal. He removed the ropes that were strangling it. Grabbing the steer by the horns, he began to lift and pull while talking soothingly to the mired beast. Soon, the animal had its breath back.

Reeves sank under the strain until he was in the mud up to his waist, but he continued heaving and lifting the animal. Slowly, the animal began to pull free from the suction of the bog. Bass repeatedly moved from the head to the flank of the animal, gradually loosening the hold of the bog. Finally, the animal was able to lunge to solid ground.

Bass waded out of the mud, scraped himself as clean as he could with his bare hands, stuffed his clothes into his saddlebags, mounted his horse and rode off stark naked, never uttering a word to the astonished cowboys.

Outlaws were overrunning the Indian Territory in 1875, robbing banks, trains, stores, post offices, as well as Indians and homesteaders. The Indian police, called "Lighthorse" because they were mounted, had no jurisdiction over the white outlaws. The only jurisdiction in these cases fell to the United States Court for the Western District of Arkansas.

It seemed ludicrous that the court's sole judge and small group of deputies were somehow expected to enforce law and order for the 75,000 square miles of outlaw-infested terrain.

Isaac C. Parker was appointed judge for the Federal Western District Court at Fort Smith, Arkansas, May 10,

1875. One of his first official acts was to appoint two hundred deputies to curb the lawlessness.

The Indian Nations had the wildest rampage of outlawry ever to happen on horseback throughout the entire southwest.

White outlaws so terrorized the Creeks and Seminoles that all whites, with or without a badge, were unwelcome. Deputies were issued "John Doe" warrants which could be served on anyone believed to be engaged in criminal activity.

Bass Reeves was an ideal choice for deputy marshal. He knew the tribal languages and the back country well. And, as a black man, he was not considered unwelcome as a white deputy would be.

Reeves carried warrants in his pockets that often totaled nine hundred dollars or more. Of this, he would net in the vicinity of four hundred dollars after he paid his expenses.

Though Reeves had never learned to read or write, Bass would have someone read the warrants to him until he memorized which name belonged to each warrant. If the man Reeves arrested could not read, then the deputy had to locate someone who could to make sure that he had the right person.

Reeves would be gone on trips lasting months. Eventually, he would arrive in Fort Smith, often single-handed, herding bands of men charged with crimes ranging from bootlegging to murder. It wasn't unusual for his belt to be shot in two, a button shot from his coat, or his hat's brim with a bullet hole through it.

His accouterments while traveling included a gourd dipper tied to his saddlebag. This he used when stopping at farmhouses for water.

Bass used a number of ruses to capture his prey. He used various styles of dress, sometimes as a cowboy, sometimes a tramp, a gunslinger or an outlaw. He also used a number of aliases. One time, Reeves trailed two train robbers with five thousand dollar rewards on their heads. He wanted those rewards.

He took an old pair of boots, lopped off their heels, selected a cane, and then shot three bullet holes in an old floppy hat. Wearing this outfit, Bass left his horse and posse members at camp and walked twenty-eight miles to the robbers' cabin.

There, he asked the mother of the two fugitives if he could rest a spell. His disguise was so effective he was asked to join the family for dinner and a good night's sleep. By morning, Bass had handcuffed the two robbers and marched them the twenty-eight miles back to the posse.

Bass refused to make exceptions in arresting his quarry. He once arrested his own son on a murder warrant after a two-week manhunt. His son was tried, convicted, and sentenced to life in prison, but was later given a full pardon.

Reeves was known by practically everyone in the Indian Nations. He even counted the bandit queen Belle Starr among his friends. Once, he stopped by her house when she had company to warn her that he was trailing Bob and Grat Dalton, of the Dalton Gang.

"Bass Reeves is one of the few deputy marshals I trust," she told Dr. Jesse Moonie, her personal physician.

The time came when Reeves was given a warrant for the arrest of Belle Starr. It was the one time in history that she turned herself in to the Fort Smith court.

Reeves killed fourteen men in his performance of duty while assigned to the federal district courts during his thirty-two year career.

When state agencies took over the deputy marshal roles after 1907, Bass Reeves, at age eighty-three, accepted a job as patrolman with the Muskogee city police department. From 1907 until 1909, there was never a crime committed on his beat.

Bass Reeves' health failed in 1909. He died of Bright's disease January 10, 1910.

CHAPTER 8

WILD BILL HICKOK

'He killed more than one hundred men'

Wild Bill Hickok was a master of the Colt Navy.

He left no doubt of this on one occasion when he walked into a saloon to have a beer. Four men at the bar, a bit inebriated and loud-mouthed, commented about Wild Bill's nose and his clothes. They obviously were not aware of his skills with a gun.

Wild Bill took offense at their remarks. When the gun smoke cleared, three of the men were dead and the other, while still alive, was missing half his chin. Bill himself was shot in the arm. That wouldn't be his last killing.

Wild Bill Hickok
1837-1876
(Google Images)

James Butler Hickok was born in Troy Grove Illinois in 1837. He left home in 1855 at nineteen years of age with his brother Lorenzo. He took a job as a stagecoach driver on the Santa Fe and Oregon Trails. Except for one two month period, he never went back home.

Hickok homesteaded 160 acres in Johnson County, Kansas, and became a constable in Monticello Township.

The legend of Wild Bill Hickok probably got its origins at Rock Creek Station, Nebraska, which was a stopover for overland stages and Pony Express riders. Hickok was a stock tender at the almost bankrupt station.

The station was previously owned by David McCanles. McCanles showed up on July 12, 1861, accompanied by James Wood and hired hand James Gordon, to collect money owed him for the sale of the station.

Wild Bill entered the station at the time an altercation was taking place. After a short argument, Hickok killed McCanles and wounded both Woods and Gordon, who later were killed, one beaten to death with a hoe by station operator Horace Wellman, and the other from a shotgun blast.

A trial was held, but it was essentially a farce. The 12-year-old son of McCanles, who witnessed the killing of his father, was not allowed to testify. Wild Bill and Wellman put forth a case of self-defense. Being employees of the Overland Stage Company, the most powerful company west of the Mississippi, Hickok and Wellman had a lot of friends.

Exaggerated accounts of the shootout appeared in newspapers, some saying Wild Bill had held off and killed ten men in a bloody one-sided fight, none of which was true. Wild Bill did not seem to object to the publicity.

Another tale that circulated about Wild Bill was that he had killed a grizzly bear with only a bowie knife and his bare hands. This is held as unlikely. Still, the story added to the wildly growing legend of Wild Bill Hickok.

It was in Springfield, Missouri where Wild Bill killed his next man. There, he shot and killed Davis K. Tutt, an

Arkansas gambler, in a street shootout. He was arrested and acquitted on the grounds of self defense.

Hickok was a U.S. Marshal at Fort Riley from 1867 to 1869. His duties were to recover stolen government property, mostly livestock, and arresting thieves and returning deserters to the army.

He led Custer's 7th Cavalry and other units against the hostile Cheyenne, Kiowa and Arapaho Indians, who had been harassing the Overland Stage. Both Wild Bill and newspaper writers greatly exaggerated this episode in Hickok's life. Hickok told lies that nobody questioned and the writers loved the Wild West image.

He was attacked by a Cheyenne war party when scouting for the 10th Cavalry and received a nasty thigh wound. He was thirty-two-years-old at the time, and it was at this point he returned home to recuperate.

Hickok was named sheriff of Ellis County, Kansas in 1869. He killed two more men there, both of whom were trying to enhance their own reputations by killing Wild Bill Hickok. Citizens of Ellis County soon voted Hickok out of office.

In 1871, Bill was appointed marshal of Abilene. There he had confrontations with outlaws Ben Thompson and John Wesley Hardin. Hardin left town when Wild Bill managed to disarm him.

Wild Bill was paid $150 a month plus a percentage of the fines. He also received fifty cents for every unlicensed dog that he shot. He generally did not take his duties seriously, and spent most of his time playing poker.

Hickok toured with Buffalo Bill's Wild West show in 1872 and 1873. He befriended Jane-Canary Burke, better known as "Calamity" Jane. While the publicity mill had them in a torrid romance, the affair appears somewhat dubious from the records. Some records indicate Wild Bill was fired from the show due to drunkenness.

Hickok gave an interview to journalist Henry M. Stanley that appeared in the *St. Louis Missouri Democrat.* He was asked by Stanley, "I say, Mr. Hickok, how many white men have you killed to our certain knowledge?"

He paused, deliberating, "I suppose I have killed considerably over a hundred."

"What made you kill all those men? Did you kill them without cause or provocation?"

"No by heaven, I never killed one man without good cause."

Wild Bill married Agnes Lake Thatcher, the owner of a circus, in Cheyenne in 1876.

Hickok finally moved to the gold rush boom town of Deadwood, South Dakota. On August 2, 1876, he sat down for a game of poker at Nuttall & Mann's No. 10 saloon. Contrary to his usual practice, Wild Bill sat with his back to the door instead of against the wall.

Jack McCall, a twenty-five-year-old drifter, shot Wild Bill in the back of the head in an effort to enhance his own reputation.

At the time he died, Hickok was holding two black aces and two black eights, which became known as the "dead man's" hand.

When tried, McCall claimed he was getting revenge for his brother who Hickok had supposedly killed in Kansas. His first trial was declared illegal as it took place in Indian Territory. In a second trial, he was convicted and hung on March 1, 1877.

Hickok's escapades were widely publicized during his career.

Brownville Advertiser (25th July, 1861

Three wagon loads of arms and ammunition passed through the neighborhood below here last week, going westward. On Friday three men were killed at Rock Creek on the Military Road about thirty or thirty five miles west of this. All we know is that the difficulty originated in the distribution of a wagon load of stuff from the Missouri river, and it is supposed it was one of the three wagons mentioned above.

During the difficulty some secessionist put a rope around a Union Man's neck, and dragged him some distance toward a tree with the avowed purpose of hanging him. He (Hickok) managed to escape.

They then gave him notice to leave in a certain time or be hung. At the end of the time five of them went to his house to see if he had gone, when he commenced firing on them and killed three out of the five; the other two making a hasty retreat.

Missouri Weekly Patriot (27th July, 1865)

David Tutt, of Yellville, Arkansas, was shot on the public square, at 6 o'clock on Friday last, by James B. Hickok, better known in Southwest Missouri as "Wild Bill." The difficulty occurred from a game of cards. Hickok is a native of Homer, Lasalle County, Illinois, and is about twenty-six years of age. He has engaged since his sixteenth year, with the exception of about two years, with Russell, Majors and Waddill, in Government service, as scout, guide, or with exploring parties, and has rendered most efficient and signal service to the Union cause, as numerous acknowledgments from the different

69

commanding offers with whom he has served will testify.

Missouri Weekly Patriot
(10ᵗʰ August, 1865

The trial of William Hickok for the killing of Davis Tutt, in the streets in this city week before last, was concluded on Saturday last, by a verdict of not guilty, rendered by the jury in about ten minutes after they retired to the jury room. The general dissatisfaction felt by the citizens of this place with the verdict in no way attaches to our able and efficient Circuit Attorney, nor to the Court. It is universally conceded that the prosecution was conducted in an able, efficient and vigorous manner.

Wild Bill Hickok was buried at Deadwood, South Dakota, along with his Sharps Rifle.

Frank Dalton, Lawman

Frank Dalton

Frank Dalton was the only one of the Dalton brothers to stay on the right side of the law.

He became a U.S. Marshal in 1884 for Judge Isaac Parker (The Hanging Judge) in Fort Smith, Arkansas.

Dalton was said to be a courageous officer who was killed while attempting to arrest three peddlers illegally running whiskey to the Indians.

Seeking vengeance, the three youngest Dalton brothers, Grat, Bob and Emmett, applied for silver stars.

Grat was appointed to fill Frank's position. Bob joined Grat as a posse man, and Emmett later became a posse man under the direction of his older brothers.

The Dalton brothers were said to be effective lawmen when chasing down wanted felons. They also became a law unto themselves by rustling herds of horses and selling them to willing buyers in Baxter Springs, Kansas.

The Dalton Gang comprised the last of the great bandit gangs in the west.

CHAPTER 9

JUDGE ROY BEAN (THE HANGING JUDGE)

'He used the butt of a pistol as a gavel'

Judge Roy Bean
1825-1903
(Google Images)

There was never another judge like Roy Bean. He was appointed justice of the peace by Pecos County Commissioners and declared himself "Law West of the Pecos". In 1882, lawlessness was so bad that the railroad asked the Texas Rangers for help. The nearest legal authority was in Fort Stockton, more than 100 miles away.

Judge Roy Bean came to the rescue. He built the "Jersey Lilly Saloon, Court Room and Pool Hall" in Langtry, Texas. His saloon was named for the actress of his dreams, Lillie Langtry, but a sign painter misspelled her name on the saloon sign.

His actions were sometimes comical, but they were also final. One time, a body found near the Pecos River was brought to Judge Bean's saloon.

73

The dead man's pockets contained forty dollars and a pistol. Judge Bean was quick to rule. He fined the dead body forty dollars for carrying a concealed weapon and took the money to reimburse the county for burial expenses.

Pencil sketch of Judge Bean's Jersey Lily saloon.   (Courtesy Artist Linda Kirkpatrick)

He kept the dead man's gun for use as a gavel, banging the gun butt on the bar to get attention.

While legend cites Judge Bean as a "hanging" judge, there is no record that he ever sentenced a man to be hung. It is believed that newspaper reporters sometimes confused Judge Bean with Judge Isaac Parker of Fort Smith, Arkansas, who sentenced 172 men to hang and actually strung up 88 of them.

Judge Bean had only three months of formal education. The only law book the Judge ever owned was the 1879 Revised Statutes of Texas. Occasionally, he used it.

His appearance was usually bedraggled. He wore a disheveled beard and a sweat-soaked bandana. His clothes were unclean. He was overweight but was feared in the courtroom for both his demeanor and his decisions.

Judge Bean could swear in both English and Spanish with the best of them, but he would not tolerate such language in his courtroom. He often levied fines just for swearing.

Those who disagreed with him considered his decisions based on racism, where ex-confederates and Irishmen were favored and non-whites were not. He kept no records of his cases and charged five dollars to conduct an inquest or to perform a marriage or divorce.

Judge Bean dished out his own brand of justice, unfettered with the legalese of most courts. Author Bob Katz described Bean's style thusly: "It was characterized by greed, prejudice, a little common sense and lots of colorful language."

One ruling dished up by Judge Bean:

> *It is the judgment of this court that you are hereby tried and convicted of illegally and unlawfully committing certain grave offenses against the peace and dignity of the State of Texas, particularly in my bailiwick. I fine you two dollars; then get the hell out of here and never show yourself in this court again. That's my rulin'."*

One of his most controversial rulings concerned the murder of a Chinese railroad worker by an Irishman. Judge Bean pored through "The Revised Statutes of Texas", turning page after page, searching for a precedent.

Finally, he brought the pistol-butt down hard on the bar and proclaimed, "Gentlemen, I find the law very explicit on murdering your fellow man, but there's nothing here about killing a chinaman (sic). Case dismissed."

When Judge Bean was about forty years old, he settled in San Antonio. He married fifteen-year-old Virginia Chavez. The couple had four children of their own and one adopted child. The marriage was an unhappy one and they divorced around 1880.

Throughout the 1870s, he peddled firewood he had cut from another man's land without permission. He sold milk that he watered down with creek water. When his buyers started noticing minnows in the milk, Roy seemed as surprised as the buyers. He engaged in other nefarious schemes and constantly dodged creditors.

When the Galveston, Harrisburg and San Antonio Railroad was extended five hundred thirty miles across the arid Chihuahuan Desert, Bean fled his marriage and left his business troubles in San Antonio.

He stopped at Vinegaroon, Texas, built a saloon, and served railroad workers whiskey from a tent. He was appointed Justice of the Peace for District 6 (then Pecos, now Val Verde County). He came highly recommended for the job by the Texas Rangers, who felt he "had what it would take to bring the law West of the Pecos."

Judge Bean later moved his saloon-courthouse to Langtry. He was his own best customer, often being drunk and disorderly. Among his clients were roughnecks, gamblers, robbers and pickpockets.

When not called to make a decision on one of the occasional cases that came his way, Judge Bean spent his time in his saloon, hoping railroad passengers would buy a drink while the train took on water. In his bar, he charged outrageous prices and often didn't get around to returning a customer's change before the train's whistle blew to call the passenger back on board.

When customers swore and demanded their change, Judge Bean simply fined them the exact amount of their change and sent them cursing to their railroad cars.

He needed income and devised a scheme to stage a world heavyweight boxing match in Langtry. Prizefighting was illegal in most states, including Texas.

He promoted the fight heavily and attracted a crowd on fight day. He met the contestants, Robert Fitzsimmons and Peter Maher at the train depot. After serving the crowd that came to see the

Lillie Langtry
(Google Images)

fight several rounds of drinks, Bean led them to a small bridge at the shore of the Rio Grande.

Bean had ordered Mexican laborers to build the bridge to a sand bar near the Mexican shore, where Texas Rangers, who were on hand to stop the fight, had no jurisdiction.

Fitzsimmons knocked Peter Maher out with a vicious right only ninety-five seconds into the fight. Bean then led the fight followers back to his saloon for more drinks.

Roy dreamed for the day that Lillie Langtry would come to Langtry and sing. He never met Miss Lillie for whom he had named his saloon, but often wrote her. She responded by sending him two pistols which he cherished until he died.

Several months after his death, the Southern Pacific stopped at Langtry, and Miss Lillie, on her way to New Orleans from San Francisco, stepped down from the train. She visited the saloon and listened as locals told her about Roy Bean.

Judge Bean was re-elected several times. Judge Bean was relieved of his duties in 1896 when the votes counted for his re-election far exceeded those eligible to vote.

He died March 19, 1903, in Del Rio, Texas after a heavy drinking bout.

CHAPTER 10

MYSTERIOUS DAVE MATHER

'He was both a horse thief and a lawman'

David Allen Mather came from a family of seafaring lawmen in Massachusetts and his ancestors had been rugged English sailors who plied the Seven Seas. Mather aspired to become a lawman himself.

He was a man of few words, a trait that gained him the nickname of "Mysterious Dave." Both of his parents died when Dave was sixteen years of age. Early on, he walked on both sides of the law.

At age twenty-two, Mather got involved in cattle rustling in Sharp County, Arkansas. A year later, he wound up in Dodge City, Kansas, where he would be both a lawman and an outlaw.

Mysterious Dave Mather
1851-?
(Google Images)

Mather was seen, too, around the saloons of Denver, Colorado. With twin Colts bulging under his coat, he would closely watch the card players at the poker tables, but he never gambled himself.

In 1879, Mather joined outlaw Dutch Henry Born in a horse-stealing ring operating in Kansas, Colorado, New Mexico and the Texas Panhandle. Both he and Born were arrested, but Mather was acquitted. Soon after, he was arrested for taking part in a train robbery near Las Vegas, New Mexico. Again he was acquitted.

He then went to the other side of the law. Mather was appointed Deputy Las Vegas Marshal.

As a deputy, he got a taste of action on January 22, 1880. Four men, including T.J. House, James West, John Dorsey, and William Randall, were in town looking for trouble.

When they entered the Close and Patterson Variety Hall, Marshal Joe Carson asked them to check their guns. They refused and a wild gunfight ensued in which Marshal Carson was killed.

Mysterious Dave Mather killed Randall and dropped West. The other two men, Dorsey and House, managed to escape. A posse found them hiding at a house in Buena Vista, north of Las Vegas.

Within hours of being placed in the Old Town Jail, vigilantes stormed the jail and took the prisoners to the windmill on the Plaza to hang. Mrs. Joe Carson opened fire, killing both men, depriving the lynchers of their hanging opportunity.

Dave Mather was then appointed Las Vegas marshal. He decided to move on after being accused of promiscuous shooting in his capacity as marshal. He served as assistant marshal in El Paso, Texas, but left after an altercation in a brothel in which he was slightly injured.

He returned to Dodge City and hired on as assistant city marshal. Dodge was now a wide open city. Gambling houses, drinking establishments, prostitution and dance halls operated in open violation of the law. It was a heated issue among Dodge City's residents.

While acting as marshal, Mather became the co-owner of the Opera House Saloon on Front Street. The city council objected to Mather's decision to turn the Opera House Saloon into a dance hall and passed an ordinance banning all dance houses.

At the same time, the council ignored the fact that a dance hall owned by Thomas Nixon was allowed to keep operating because of its remote location. Nixon and Mather battled to put each other out of business.

A crowning blow to Mather was when the city government elected to make Thomas Nixon city marshal, replacing Mysterious Dave. This brought the feud between the two to a head. On July 18, 1884, Nixon drew a gun and fired at Mather. Mather was only sprayed by a few splinters.

Three days later, Mather approached Nixon from behind and fired four bullets into his back, killing him instantly. He was later heard to say, "I ought to have killed him six months ago."

Mather was acquitted of the murder. However, when he killed another man the following year, he was run out of town by Marshal Bill Tilghman. Mather served as a lawman in a couple of small towns in Kansas and Nebraska, but then went to San Francisco, where he took a ship to Vancouver.

He enlisted in the Royal Canadian Mounted Police, proving his prowess with both his marksmanship and his horsemanship. He was still wearing the RCMP uniform as late as 1920.

CHAPTER 11

FRED LAMBERT

'New Mexico's youngest Marshal'

Sworn in at age 16, Fred Lambert was the youngest Territorial Marshal from New Mexico.

Lambert was born in room number 31 of the famous St. James Hotel in Cimarron, New Mexico. It was a blustery winter night with a blizzard blowing outside. A hotel guest laughingly commented that he should be named "Cyclone Dick."

Henri and Mary Lambert went along with the guest's suggestion, and the guest was then asked to be Fred's godfather, which he accepted.

So, Charles Fred "Cyclone" Lambert was born in 1887. His godfather was Buffalo Bill Cody, who would later give his godchild lessons in the use of guns when he grew older. These lessons may have kept Fred alive during his law enforcement duties.

Fred Lambert
1887-1971
In a 1968 photo depicting all of the law enforcement badges he wore during his career. (Photo by Samuel McWhorter.)

Fred's father Henri, who came from Bordeaux, France, was once the personal chef of President Abraham Lincoln.

He built Lambert's Inn in Cimarron, New Mexico in 1872 and later renamed it the St. James Hotel. The hotel became a notorious gathering site during the bawdy days of the old west.

Guests at the hotel were a Who's Who of the West, including Wyatt Earp, Bat Masterson, Jesse James, Black Jack Ketchum and Clay Allison. During the saloon's heydey, twenty seven men were killed there.

During the 1870s, a favorite expression in Cimarron was, "Who was killed at Lambert's last night?" and, "It appears Lambert had himself another man for breakfast."

When the dining area of the hotel was remodeled in 1902 by the Lambert sons, four hundred bullet holes were counted in the ceiling. A double layer of heavy wood prevented anyone in the sleeping rooms upstairs from being killed. Today, the dining room ceiling still holds twenty-two bullet holes.

Fred, at age fifteen, took a job as a freight wagon driver on the route between Cimarron and Taos. At about the same time, he took a job with the Indian police. One of his first assignments was keeping peace at Picuris Peak near the Taos Pueblo.

Fred, working with two other deputies, watched as a train of mules and six men came down the trail. The train was loaded with whiskey. When Fred approached them, the leader, a man named Juan Gallegos, drew his gun. Fred was too quick. He grabbed Gallegos' gun around the cylinder at the same time that the hammer came down, smashing the web of his Fred's hand.

With his other hand, Lambert pulled his own gun and struck Gallegos between the eyes. The deputies operating with Fred arrested the entire gang.

Early in his lawman career, Fred was befriended by a man named Frank Harrington, the man who shot Black Jack Ketchum. Frank took Fred out behind the walls of the Cimarron jail and taught him how to shoot.

By the time Fred became sheriff of Cimarron, the town's wild days were over. As Fred walked the streets at night, the worst thing he might have to deal with was taking care of a drunken "Bunny" Alpers.

Alpers was Cimarron's mayor and had a well-known habit of Saturday night binges. When Bunny passed out at the tavern, the bar keeper would hang an old red railroad lantern on the porch. This was a signal for Fred to come and help Bunny to his house.

Fred would load him in a wheelbarrow and haul him home, dumping him in front of his house.

Lambert was an active rancher. He took an interest in the restoration of the Aztec Mill, which was built in 1864 by Lucien B. Maxwell, of the Maxwell Land Grant. Fred operated it as a tourist attraction for many years.

Fred Lambert also wrote poetry, published and contributed to several books, and made pen and ink drawings and paintings.

The Mason County War

Scott Cooley

The Mason County War in Texas began with the shooting of Ted Williamson. It became a confrontation that lasted more than a year and claimed a dozen lives.

Williamson had been arrested for stealing livestock. He was abducted and shot to death by his enemies.

A friend of Williamson's, Scott Cooley, believed that Sheriff John Worley, who was escorting Williamson to jail when he was shot, was in collusion with the ambushers.

Cooley avenged Williamson's murder by shooting Worley and cutting off his ears.

CHAPTER 12

CHRIS MADSEN

'He was one of The Three Guardsmen'

Chris Madsen
1851-1944
He was one of the "Three Guardsmen of Oklahoma."
(Photo from Google Images)

Chris Madsen was one of a trio of lawmen known as "The Three Guardsmen". The other two were Heck Thomas and Bill Tilghman. The three were credited with wiping out organized crime in Oklahoma.

One hot and humid night in the town of El Reno, Oklahoma, gunshots crashed through the window glass of the home of Deputy U.S. Marshal Chris Madsen. The bullets struck close to the sleeping Madsen's head but bored into the wall above him. Madsen dropped to the floor, crawled to the door and opened it just enough to see the two assassins darting to the trees. Madsen fired his revolver and was rewarded by a scream. When a second figure moved through the shadows, Madsen fired again. The man groaned as he went down.

The two would-be assassins were paid killers who were hired to kill Marshal Madsen because he was making life miserable for whiskey peddlers in the Territory.

Madsen's handling of the two outlaws was typical of his brand of handing out justice: "Shoot first and ask questions later."

Chris Madsen became a lawman at the behest of, a prominent businessman of Kingfisher, Oklahoma. William Grimes was asked to accept the post of U.S. Marshal for the Territory of Oklahoma. Grimes accepted, but soon found it was no easy task to induce young men to leave their homes to hunt outlaws. Grimes asked the commandant of Fort Riley for help.

"My best man for you would be Chris Madsen," the commandant told Grimes, adding it would be no problem to release him from army duty early.

Grimes approached Madsen. Madsen told him in his broken English with a Danish accent that he was a soldier, not a peace officer.

"The pay is two hundred and fifty dollars a month, Madsen, think it over."

For Madsen, whose army pay was twenty-nine dollars a month, the figure sounded mind-boggling.

"I'll take it," Madsen decided, "I know mama (his wife) will like it."

The big Dane acted quickly to let the Territory know a new lawman was on duty.

Madsen learned that whiskey was being peddled to the Indians from Fort Reno. One night, Madsen waited near a creek close to the fort.

Suddenly, he saw five men charging toward him. Madsen's marksmanship soon convinced the charging men to surrender. They proved to be two soldiers and three civilians.

Madsen immigrated to the United States in 1870. He became Quartermaster Sergeant of the Fifth Cavalry and had charge of the Indian Scouts. Madsen fought in nearly every Indian campaign in Arizona, Wyoming, Nebraska, Dakota, Idaho, Utah, Colorado and Montana before becoming President Chester Arthur's guide to the Yellowstone in 1883.

He then "retired" to become Quartermaster Sergeant in the Field in the Twin Territories. These were the Oklahoma and Indian territories, located between the Missouri River and the Rocky Mountains. In 1907, the two regions were combined to form the state of Oklahoma, the forty-sixth state in the Union.

Madsen settled on a homestead near El Reno, Oklahoma. Outlaws were making life so miserable for people in the territories that Madsen became a deputy marshal, earning a reputation as "a fighter who never showed the white feather".

Roaming the Indian Territory was a figure known as the Dutchman. He went about the Territory daring anyone to arrest him. He was armed to the teeth with pistols and a rifle and terrorized anyone near him. He was also considered to be a notorious horse-thief.

When the Dutchman was arrested and jailed by three officers in Oklahoma City, he caused so much commotion that city officials asked that he be moved to a Federal jail in Guthrie, Oklahoma.

U.S. Marshal Grimes assigned Madsen to move the prisoner from Oklahoma City to Guthrie. While Madsen had no trouble transporting the prisoner, several days later The Dutchman escaped from the Guthrie jail

The Dutchman broke into a Norman, Oklahoma store to steal supplies. He was discovered by a local officer and shot in the stomach. Again, Madsen was called to get the man. He found him dying on the banks of the South Canadian River, about four miles from Norman.

One time, Madsen was called to escort a judge on his rounds. At Beaver, Oklahoma, they found lodging in a popular saloon. Their room was on the second floor, directly above the saloon.

During the night, drunken cowboys began firing pistols into the ceiling, which just happened to be the floor of Madsen's rented room. Madsen went down to the saloon to corral the exuberant cowboys.

One of the cowboys shouted, "I'm a wild son-of-a-bitch from Cripple Creek!"

Madsen said, "I knew who you were, I just didn't know where you were from."

In one case, Madsen met an informant that told him Felix Young, a train robber, was out on the street. Madsen approached the wanted man, but the outlaw recognized him and ran for a nearby horse.

Madsen fired five quick shots and killed the horse. The big Dane then ran down the wanted man and took him into custody.

Still another case involved Red Buck George Waightman, a member of the Doolin and Dalton gangs. Waightman was hiding in a dugout near Cheyenne. A posse, including Madsen, surrounded the dugout, and called for the outlaw to come out with his hands up.

When Waightman began firing, Madsen is said to have fired a single rifle shot, and as the old timers described it, "Waightman's case was automatically appealed to a higher court."

Chris Madsen was the most cosmopolitan of all of Oklahoma's pioneer officers, according to Gordon Hines, author of the *Oklahombres: Particularly the Wilder Ones*. Madsen was born at Copenhagen, Denmark February 25, 1851. He joined the Danish Army and served in the Danish-Prussian and Franco-Prussian wars and in the Foreign Legion in Algeria.

After arriving in the U.S., he served some time as a scout and gained considerable knowledge of the west while hunting buffalo.

First Sheriff of San Francisco

John Coffey Hays
(California State Library)

John Coffey Hays, known as Jack Hays, developed a reputation as a gunman who would fight to uphold the law.

When the Texas Rangers were formed in 1840, Hays was elected a major in the group. He served in the Rangers for ten years and then moved to California where he became wealthy from his real estate investments.

He purchased a huge tract of land across the Bay from San Francisco. This land later became the site for the City of Oakland.

Hays became the first sheriff of San Francisco County (1850-53) and brought about many police reforms.

CHAPTER 13

JOHN HORTON SLAUGHTER

'Only five-foot-six, he looked tall to outlaws'

John Slaughter stood barely five-foot-six-inches tall, but outlaws still froze when confronted with his steely black eyes. A fellow lawman once described Slaughter thusly: "He was like a spider spinning its web for the unwary fly."

When Slaughter told a man, "Lay down or be shot down," his lips barely moved, but few outlaws dared challenge his order.

Some residents of Cochise County, Arizona, maintained that John Horton Slaughter sometimes killed fugitives and

John Horton Slaughter
1841-1922
(Google Images)

then neglected to report their deaths. Since the sheriff carried out these acts alone, such reports cannot be proven or disproven.

James Wolf, who worked sometimes as a deputy sheriff, recounted one visit that Slaughter made to his ranch while in pursuit of an outlaw. Two days later, he returned leading the wanted man's horse, but with no prisoner.

Wolf surmised that Slaughter had insisted on fighting it out with the outlaw rather than risk his escaping during the trip back to Tombstone.

"Slaughter was killing these bad men just as they had killed so many victims, but on even terms...At all times they had an even break from the sheriff," Ford is quoted in the book, *Desert Lawmen: The High Sheriffs of New Mexico and Arizona.*

Another writer, Walter Noble Burns, took the issue even further in his book, *Tombstone: An Iliad of the Southwest,* saying that a sort of law enforcement "decadence" set in after the departure of the Wyatt Earp posse:

> *This decadent period was notable for a lax administration of law and the absence of strong men at the helm of public affairs. Crime flourished as never before...The criminals were pestiferously active. It was an age of thieves rather than bandits...Though they operated on a small scale, they kept eternally at it...Criminals were showing a disposition to organize. Tombstone was their headquarters, and the town was gradually passing under their domination.*

Slaughter was born in Louisiana October 2, 1841. He was often decorated for his duties as a Texas Ranger before becoming a prominent cattleman in Cochise County. He and his brothers, who owned various cattle partnerships, drove cattle herds to New Mexico, Kansas, Mexico and California. Along the way, they picked up "strays" whenever they could.

Cochise County administrators sought a man with the force and courage to handle a serious situation, even if he had to adopt extralegal measures. This man, said Burns, was Sheriff John H. Slaughter.

Slaughter imposed law and order with his six-shooter, repeating shotgun and Henry rifle when he wasn't participating in an all-night poker game. In those days, he spent more time playing poker than he did raising cattle or chasing outlaws.

His favorite card-playing pigeon was the famous cattle king, John Chisum, a notoriously bad poker player. Slaughter delighted in beating Chisum out of a few head of his choice beef cattle.

He especially enjoyed bluffing. He would bet as much on a pair of deuces as on a straight flush. He always paid off in coin or paper. He was known to have lost pots as high as five hundred dollars. If he suspected anyone of cheating, he might suddenly pull his pistol and relieve the entire party of its gambling stakes.

Slaughter was playing poker one night against a suspected cattle rustler named Barney Gallagher, and a couple of other cowboys. The sheriff noticed Gallagher was playing with marked cards. When Gallagher began to rake in the largest pot of the night, he found himself staring into the muzzle of Slaughter's .45 pistol.

The Sheriff swept up the pot, backed out the door, mounted his horse and galloped off. Gallagher followed him to where Slaughter's cattle were grazing on John Chisum's ranch. There, he confronted Slaughter's foreman.

"You tell that midget sonofabitch I'm here to kill him."

"Wait here, I'll tell him what you said," the foreman rode off, chuckling to himself.

Gallagher waited with a shotgun across his lap as Slaughter appeared on the horizon. When the sheriff came within range, Gallagher raised his shotgun. A shot from Slaughter gun tore through Gallagher before he could position his shotgun. He died, with blood pumping from the hole in his heart.

Another time, Slaughter played poker for three straight days above Jim Graham's saloon. His opponents were master swindlers. The sexy woman tending bar kept sending both new cards and fresh drinks to the table.

She was working double duty for the crooks. She was not only marking the new cards she sent to the table, but she was spiking Slaughter's drinks. Slaughter lost a small fortune.

Slaughter was elected sheriff of Cochise County in 1886. The area was infested with rustlers and highwaymen. One case was that of the Jack Taylor Gang. Four of Taylor's men were still running loose after a train holdup in the Mexican state of Sonora.

The four men were Geronimo Miranda, Manuel Robles, Nieves Deron and Fred Federico. They were wanted by both the Mexican Rurales and by Arizona authorities.

The thieves made their mistake by returning to Tombstone where they had relatives. By hiding there, they were also hiding right under the nose of the law, which was John Slaughter.

Slaughter received information that the gang was holed up in the home of Flora Cardenas. The sheriff and his deputies staked out the adobe home. Someone was able to tip off the bandits that they were being watched and they disappeared.

Sheriff Slaughter tracked them to Clifton, Arizona, and then to Wilcox, Arizona. His network of Spanish-speaking tipsters told him that Manuel Robles' brother, Guadeloupe Robles, had a firewood business in a town called Contention. Slaughter took his posse to Contention.

When they stormed the house of Guadeloupe, they found Manuel Robles and Nieves Deron asleep.

"To your feet," Slaughter ordered. "Get up, with your hands high." Instead of obeying, the outlaws came up shooting.

Slaughter quickly killed Guadeloupe, the woodcutter, who up to then was guilty of only harboring the outlaws. Manuel Robles and Nieves Deron darted for the rocks. Deron kept firing from the rocks, with one bullet clipping the lobe of Slaughter's right ear.

Slaughter's next shot hit and killed Deron. Robles, wounded and bleeding, escaped into a thicket.

This was the end of the Jack Taylor gang. Jack Taylor was arrested by Mexican authorities and was serving life in prison. Deron had confessed, while dying, that he had shot and killed the engineer of the train robbed in Sonora. Robles and Miranda were later shot in a running gun battle with the Mexican Rurales in the Sierra Madre Mountains of Mexico.

Federico thought he was shooting at Sheriff Slaughter when he mistook Deputy Sheriff Cesario Lucero for the lawman, whom he shot and killed. He was captured soon after .

When John Slaughter eventually retired to his San Bernardino Ranch near Douglas, Arizona, his feet had become so swollen he had to wear slippers and often used crutches. His feebleness progressed to the point he could not recall the names of the cards when he sat down to play poker with his grandson. He also developed high blood pressure.

He died February 15, 1922 when he visited his beloved San Bernardino ranch for the last time.

CHAPTER 14

JUDGE ISAAC C. PARKER

'The Hanging Judge'

Judge Isaac
Parker
1838-1896
(Signal Corps,
National Archives

On September 3, 1875, six men slowly walked onto the Fort Smith gallows. Five thousand people squeezed in to watch as the men's death warrants were announced.

Hangman George Maledon placed a rope around each man's neck, tying a knot behind the left ear—a method devised to snap the neck and ease the suffering. Maledon then draped black hoods over their heads and walked to the end of the wooden platform.

There were three whites, two Indians, and one Negro among the six felons.

Within seconds, he grabbed the lever releasing the trap. The men fell five and a half feet, cracking their necks when they stopped.

The above description is the way Roger H. Tuller described one of the hangings ordered by Judge Parker in his book, *Let No Guilty Man Escape.*

Sentencing six men to hang quickly labeled Judge Parker as "The Hanging Judge," not only in Arkansas but throughout the U.S. and the world.

At the age of thirty six, Parker was the youngest Federal judge in the west. Holding court for the first time on May 10, 1875, eight men were found guilty of murder and sentenced to death.

Judge Parker held court six days a week, often spending up to ten hours a day trying defendants.

In all, Judge Isaac Parker sentenced one hundred sixty one men to death. Seventy nine of them were hanged. The news of the 1875 hanging spread quickly across the country announcing a new era of justice in Arkansas and the West.

Yet, Parker was not considered a cruel man. He was hard on killers and rapists. He reserved his sympathy for the victim and his family. Most of his critics lived in civilized communities and did not appreciate the raw frontier conditions of the Indian Territory.

With his mind set on bringing law and order to the area, Judge Parker told U.S. Marshal James F. Fagan to hire two hundred deputies. He wanted them to bring in all the robbers, murderers and thieves they could find.

None of his capital cases caused Judge Parker as much exasperation as did the leather-faced miscreant Belle Starr. To stay out of court she bribed and sometimes seduced his deputies.

She had a consuming passion for gunslingers and bandits. She had been a mistress of outlaw Cole Younger, a member of the James gang. She had been the wife successively of a horse thief and of the Cherokee outlaw Sam Starr.

She boasted to a reporter, "I am a friend to any brave and gallant outlaw."

Belle acted as an organizer, planner and fence for rustlers, horse thieves and bootleggers, who distilled and sold whiskey to the Indians.

Belle Starr was one of Judge Parker's biggest Headaches. (Google Images)

When Parker did finally manage to incarcerate her for nine months for stealing horses from her neighbors, her lawyers went over Parker's head to the White House, which commuted her sentence. Belle was shot and killed in an ambush in 1889, probably by her newest husband.

The thing that bothered Judge Parker most during his time on the court was the Supreme Court reversals of capital crimes tried in Fort Smith. Fully two thirds of the cases appealed to the higher court were reversed and sent back to Fort Smith for new trials.

The Hangman, George Maledon, was a small mean-looking German who looked forward to executing the verdict. Pardons and appeals cheated Maledon of his fun in more than half of the cases.

Maledon was almost as skilled in handling a gun as he was with the rope. He shot down five men sentenced to death while they were trying to escape.

The only court with jurisdiction over the Indian Territory was the U.S. Court for the Western District of Arkansas located in Fort Smith, Arkansas.

Reminiscent of Abraham Lincoln, Parker was born in a log cabin on Oct. 15, 1838. He had an early appetite for knowledge and paid for his higher education by teaching children in a country primary school. At age 17, he decided to study law.

101

He passed the bar in 1859, and began a law practice in St. Joseph, Mo., quickly developing a reputation as an honest lawyer. In 1860, he was elected city attorney. By the end of the decade, he was a judge for the 12th Missouri Circuit.

Parker then decided to run for the U.S. House of Representatives, which he easily won when his opponent withdrew two weeks before the election. By the end of his second term, Parker sensed the political atmosphere in his district had changed, and he began lobbying for a presidential appointment to an office.

President Ulysses S. Grant appointed him to succeed William Story as federal court judge for the Western District of Arkansas. The bench was vacant because Story had been impeached for bribery.

"People have said to me, 'You are the judge who hung so many men,' and I always answer: 'It is not I who has hung them. I never hung a man. It is the law,'" Parker said.

Under federal law at the time, death sentences were automatic for rape or murder convictions. Only 2.5 percent of Parker's cases involved capital crimes, even though that became his legend.

In twenty one years on the bench, Judge Parker tried thirteen thousand four hundred ninety cases. Three hundred-forty-four were capital crimes. Nine-thousand-four-hundred-fifty-four cases resulted in guilty pleas. One hundred and sixty men were sentenced to death by hanging.

Only seventy nine of them were actually hung. The rest died in jail, appealed or were pardoned.

In his instructions to a jury, Parker told them, "Do equal and exact justice...Permit no innocent man to be punished, but let no guilty man escape."

Still, Parker claimed the death penalty should be abolished. Near the end of his life, Parker said, "I am the most misunderstood and misrepresented of men. Misrepresented because misunderstood."

Parker's jurisdiction began to shrink as more courts were given authority over parts of the Indian Territory. In September, Congress closed the court. Six weeks after the court was closed, on November 17, 1896 Parker died of a heart attack.

The Buck Gang

The Buck Gang included, l to r, Naomi July, Sam Sampson, Rufus Buck, Lucky Davis and Lewis Davis.
(Google Images)

The Buck gang was made up of five illiterate Indians who terrorized the Old Indian Territory of Arkansas-Oklahoma. The gang was led by Rufus Buck.

The first woman taken by the gang was a widow named Wilson who was riding in a wagon when the gang came upon her. All five men raped her, then took her shoes away and shot at her feet as they fled.

In another incident, the gang raided the house of Henry Hassan. While they held him under guard, all five men raped his wife.

The five men appeared before Judge Isaac Parker, who sentenced them to hang on October 31, 1895. They appealed to the U.S. Supreme Court which refused to hear the case. The men were rescheduled to hang on July 1, 1896. The five men were all hung at the same time.

CHAPTER 15

'DOC' HOLLIDAY

He had a natural ability for gambling

"Doc" Holliday
1851-1887
(Google Images)

After fulfilling all of the education requirements, the degree of Doctor of Dental Surgery was conferred on John Henry "Doc" Holliday on March 1, 1872.

He was a good dentist, but soon after he started his own practice, Doc discovered he had tuberculosis.

He consulted a number of medical opinions, and the consensus all gave Doc only a few months to live. He was advised to find a drier climate.

Doc packed his bags and headed west, riding to the end of the railroad line, which at the time was Dallas, Texas. Again he opened a dental office, but a hacking cough from his tuberculosis infection would erupt in the middle of his treating a patient. He simply couldn't practice dentistry.

Doc soon learned that he had a natural ability for gambling. This became his sole means of support.

Holiday knew that the gambler who could not protect himself would soon be a dead gambler. He practiced daily with his six-gun and knife.

It wasn't long before he had an argument with a saloon keeper named Austin. The argument soon flared into violence. Each man pulled his pistol and several shots were fired, but not one struck its intended target.

Both shooters were arrested. Most of the citizens who read about the account in the *Dallas Weekly Herald* found the incident amusing. They changed their minds, however, when a short time later, Doc put two large holes through a prominent citizen, killing him.

Doc was forced to flee Dallas a short distance ahead of a posse. He rode to Jacksboro and found a job dealing Faro. Jacksboro was a tough cowtown situated near an army post.

Holliday now carried a gun in a shoulder holster, one on his hip, and a long, wicked knife as well. Each day he was becoming more expert with each of the weapons. He continued his argumentative ways and became embroiled in three more gunfights. In one, he left another man dead.

In his next shooting confrontation he made the mistake of killing a soldier. This killing brought the U.S. Government into the investigation. Doc lit out again, knowing that his back trail would be crowded with the Army, U.S. Marshals, Texas Rangers and local lawmen.

Heading for Colorado, eight hundred miles away, Doc stopped for short periods at Pueblo, Georgetown and Central City. He killed three more men before he reached Denver.

In Denver, he used the alias of Tom Mackey, keeping relatively unknown until he became involved in a ruckus with Bud Ryan, a Faro dealer at Babbitt's House. He came very near to cutting Ryan's head off in this fight. Although his victim didn't die, public resentment sent him packing again.

He went to Wyoming, then New Mexico and finally to Fort Griffin, Texas. There, he met the only woman with whom he was ever known to associate. She was known as "Big Nose" Kate, a frontier dance hall woman and prostitute.

She liked her job as both a madam and a prostitute. She belonged to no man or no Madam's house, plying her trade however she chose.

It was in Fort Griffin that Holliday also met Wyatt Earp. Earp was on the trail of Dave Rudabaugh and was seeking information about his whereabouts. While Doc was helping Earp get the information he needed, they became fast friends.

A bully named Ed Bailey sat down one day to play in a poker game in which Holliday was playing. In an obvious attempt to irritate Holliday, Bailey kept picking up the discards and looking through them. This was against a rigid rule in western poker, and anyone who did so forfeited the pot.

Holliday warned Bailey twice. Bailey ignored him. When, in the very next hand Bailey picked up the discards again, Doc reached out and raked in the pot without showing his hand.

Bailey brought a six shooter from under the table, while a large knife materialized in Doc's hand. Before Bailey could pull the trigger, Doc disemboweled him.

This time, Doc felt he was well within the law and stuck around town and allowed himself to be arrested. Once he was locked up Bailey's friends and the town vigilantes clamored for his blood.

"Big Nose" Kate knew Doc was a goner unless someone did something quick. Kate took action. She set a fire to an old shed. It burned so hotly it threatened to engulf the town.

Everyone in town went to fight the fire except for three people, Kate, Doc and the officer who guarded him. Kate stepped in front of the startled guard with a pistol in her hand. She then passed the pistol to Doc and the two fled into the night, hiding in the brush to avoid the search parties.

Doc felt he owed Kate something for what she did. The next morning they headed for Dodge City. Doc gave up gambling and hung out his dentist's shingle. Kate gave up being a prostitute and inhabiting the saloons.

Kate stood the boredom of respectable living as long as she could. Then she told Doc she was going back to the bright lights and excitement of the dance halls and gambling dens.

After their split-up, Doc went back to dealing Faro in the Long Branch Saloon. A group of Texas cowboys, who had just arrived in Dodge City with a herd of cattle, were ready to live it up.

Word came into the Long Branch that several of the trail drivers had Wyatt Earp cornered and were ready to shoot him down. Doc leaped through the door with a gun in his hand.

When he arrived on the scene, two cowboys named Morrison and Driscoll were holding cocked revolvers on Wyatt, goading him to draw or be shot down. About twenty other of their cowboy friends stood nearby, taunting and insulted the enraged, but helpless, Wyatt.

When Doc unloosed a volume of profanity, the self-styled bad men turned toward him. Earp rapped Morrison over the head with his long-barreled Colt. He then went about disarming the other cowboys. Wyatt never forgot the fact that Doc Holliday saved his life that night in Dodge City.

Eventually, Doc decided to go to Tombstone. Unknown to him, this is the same destination that Wyatt and the rest of the Earp clan were headed. Morgan was coming in from Montana, Wyatt and James from Dodge City, and

Virgil from Prescott, where he had just been made a Deputy U.S. Marshal.

Virgil Earp deputized Doc Holliday during the Earp brothers shootout at which is now called the "Gunfight at the O.K. Corral". This the only time that Holliday was a true law enforcement officer. Three men died in the shootout. Holliday was said to have a bullet in each of them.

Holliday, at age thirty five, moved to Glenwood Springs, Colorado. He passed away from his debilitating disease November 8, 1887. He is buried in Linwood Cemetery.

The Hanging Judge's 'Hangman'

George Maledon

Someone had to do it. When a felon was convicted and sentenced to hang by Judge Isaac Parker, *The Hanging Judge*, it was George Maledon that acted as executioner.

Maledon was a member of the Fort Smith, Arkansas police department. For additional income, he offered to act as hangman.

He took pride in his hangman's work. He prepared carefully for each execution, oiling and stretching the ropes to assure a "drop" that quickly and neatly killed the condemned.

He considered multiple executions a particular challenge and had a twelve-man gallows erected.

For twenty-one years, Maledon hanged almost all of the seventy-nine men condemned to death by Judge Parker.

CHAPTER 16

BURT MOSSMAN

Burt Mossman was a cattle rustler's nightmare. At sixteen years of age, he got his first job as a cowboy. By age twenty one, he was foreman for a New Mexico ranch running eight thousand head of cattle.

Burton Mossman
1867-1956
(Google Images)

Burt then took the job of managing the giant Aztec Cattle Company, better known as the Hash Knife outfit, which ran sixty thousand head of cattle. The company was about to go bankrupt because of cattle rustlers.

On his first day on the job, a foreman met Burt with more news of stolen cattle. The two men followed the trail and captured three rustlers. This ended Mossman's first day on the job.

His next act for the Hash Knife was to fire fifty-two of the eighty-four cowboys. These fifty-two were suspected of either rustling or helping rustlers to the Aztec Land Company's cattle.

When the company finally went bankrupt, Mossman set himself up in the butcher business.

The Arizona legislature was getting many complaints about train robbers, murders, cattle rustlers and horse thieves. Citizens of Arizona wanted some type of peace-keeping organization. Governor Nathan Oakes Murphy called Mossman to his office. He asked him to enlist peace officers for the new Arizona Rangers.

"I want no part of this, Governor. I'm on my way to making some money for the first time in my life. Besides, you can find a dozen good men for the job."

"All right," the Governor replied, "but please help draft the Bill."

That same day, Mossman contacted Frank Cox, chief attorney for the Southern Pacific Railroad in Phoenix, and the two men locked themselves in a room at the Adams Hotel until midnight.

Later, they presented to Governor Murphy a bill that was hurriedly sent to the Territorial Secretary for presentation to the Legislature. On March 21, 1901, the Legislature created the Arizona Rangers.

The Rangers were to consist of one captain at a salary of a hundred and twenty dollars a month, one sergeant at seventy-five dollars a month, and not more than twelve privates at fifty-five dollars a month.

When Mossman prepared to return to his butcher business, he was pressured at great length to take over the captaincy of the Rangers.

Finally, he said, "I suppose you'll never let me alone until I do," he said.

"That's right," replied his old friend Colonel Bill Greene, for whom Burt had once worked as a ranch manager. All of those gathered in the Governor's office agreed.

"I know the power of some of these political thugs," Mossman told the group. "I want to write my own ticket, hire my own men, take orders from nobody, and name my successor. Also, I'll take it for a year only, but I doubt that I'll live that long."

Governor Murphy readily agreed with Mossman's conditions.

Burt picked his men with skill. He selected Dayton Graham, a Bisbee peace officer and a brave man as his sergeant. His second choice was Burt Grover, who at times acted in the capacity of sergeant.

Once the roster was filled, Mossman addressed his men.

"First, I want to say that whatever you do I'll stick by you to the end. Second, our first problem is to break up the gangs moving from Sonora into our country and stealing everything they can lay their hands on."

The Arizona Rangers' first job came when the wires flashed a notice that a gang had held up a post office at Tucumcari in eastern New Mexico. The gang had killed a young boy who was simply a bystander.

Captain Mossman took four Rangers and rushed to Clifton, Arizona by special train. They then rode to the rough country around Blue Powder River. The hotly-pursued bandits, led by Bill Daniels, crossed the New Mexico border into Arizona.

For some reason, Daniels had left the group, but the remaining five outlaws continued in the direction where Mossman and his men waited. A local rancher informed Burt that the outlaw camp had been sighted.

At dawn, Mossman and his four Rangers closed in and demanded the bandits surrender. Two of the men were arrested, while the other three escaped. One of the three that escaped was soon captured, and the other two were killed from ambush.

One day in October Mossman received bad news. One of his Rangers had been killed by the Bill Smith gang. Another Ranger had been critically wounded.

113

Burt summoned one of his Rangers to go with him to Clifton. There they rode to the forks of the Black River where the fight had occurred. Burt learned from Henry Barrett, a member of the Ranger posse, the true story of what had happened.

The outlaw gang had held up a Union Pacific Train in Utah, then stolen some horses and headed south. They had holed up in a cabin on the Black River. When the leader of the posse ordered the gang to surrender, Bill Smith, the gang leader dashed to the safety of the cabin.

His brother raised his hands in a pretence of surrendering, dropping his rifle in the snow. "All right, over this way," ordered Ranger Carlos Tefio. The outlaw walked forward, slowly dragging the rifle along with a foot in the carrying strap.

When the outlaw reached a shallow draw, he pretended to fall, grabbed his rifle and shot Tefio through the stomach. Ranger Maxwell ordered Bill Smith in the cabin to surrender. Smith answered by firing a rifle shot through Maxwell's hat.

When Maxwell again peered from his hiding place, Bill Smith fired again, killing the Ranger with a bullet in the eye.

The gang leader then crossed into Mexico at Douglas, Arizona. He suspected if he stayed in Arizona he would be recognized. When he learned that no one any longer suspected his whereabouts, he returned to Douglas to enjoy the nightlife.

One evening, Ranger Dayton Graham was chatting with the night marshal when a storekeeper approached, saying a suspicious looking man was seated on the steps of his store. He wanted him removed.

When the two officers walked up to the man, the stranger produced a pistol and fired, sending a bullet through the marshal's neck. Before Graham could draw, the man fired again, shooting Graham in the lung and in the arm.

It was thought that Graham was dying. Mossman gathered Graham's family and rushed them the thirty miles to Douglas. Graham lay bedridden for two months but he did not die.

"I'll get that sonofabitch some day, Captain," he told Mossman. When he regained his health, he rode from town to town, visiting one bar after another, looking for the stranger who had shot him.

One night, he hit pay dirt. He saw his man seated at a monte table. The man immediately went for his gun, but Ranger Graham's gun spoke first. One slug tore through the man's head and two others followed into his stomach.

"That'll make sure you'll kill no more law officers, you sonofabitch," Graham hissed.

Captain Mossman arrived the next morning. Everyone was surprised when the dead man turned out to be gang leader Bill Smith.

One time Mossman chased the Mexican bandit Salivaras across the cactus-covered desert until the outlaw's horse died. Salivaras then buried himself up to his chin under a bush. He was found by Captain Mossman's dogs. Shots were exchanged. Mossman was hit in the side, but lived. Salivaras was hit in the chest and did not.

Burton Mossman re-entered the cattle business as owner of the large Diamond A ranch near Roswell, New Mexico. The five-foot ten inch Mossman continued being quick-tempered and firm, but was respected by all who worked with him.

Mossman got the Arizona Rangers off to a good start and was responsible for clearing Arizona Territory of many of its most wild and lawless.

He died September 5, 1956 at his ranch in Roswell.

CHAPTER 17

'BEAR RIVER' TOM SMITH

Abilene, Kansas had gone through two years of terror as trail-driving cowboys seeking excitement shot up their town. The out-of-town cowboys openly taunted the administrators of local city government.

What Abilene needed was a peace officer with moxie enough to stand up to these brash cowboys. One of the first seekers of the job was Tom Smith, who traveled from Colorado to apply.

Mayor Theodore C. Henry wasn't impressed with the looks of Smith, a

Tom Smith
1830-1870
(Google Images)

one-hundred-seventy pound red-head of Irish descent. The job went unfilled for months, while local volunteers tried unsuccessfully to curb the violent cowboys.

Finally, Mayor Henry relented and decided to give the job to Tom Smith. "Bear River" Tom was hired June 4, 1870 at a wage of $150. Smith was the entire police force.

Little is known about Smith's early beginnings. It is believed that he was a policeman in New York City and a bare-knuckle boxer. These theories have not been documented.

As a teenager, he was attacked by three hoodlums from the riverfront of New York. Tom gave them such a thrashing that he was brought to the attention of boxing promoter John Woods. Woods taught him the art of prizefighting and Tom became a good boxer.

Every morning he would train at the gym on Union Square, learning the finer points of the boxing game. He fought in the ring for five years until the death of his mother and father, both in the same year of 1860.

One of the first documented accounts attributed to Tom Smith was in 1868 in the town of Bear River, Wyoming. He worked for the Union Pacific Railroad. The hard-drinking and rowdy railroad workers were causing so much trouble that a vigilante committee was formed.

The vigilantes hung three of the railroad workers and made a number of other random arrests. This caused a revolt by the railroad workers who then tried to burn the local jail.

During the melee, the vigilantes hid in a log cabin and began taking sniper shots at the rioting workers. A bullet hit one of Tom Smith's friends. Enraged over the act, Smith pulled a gun and charged the log cabin.

Smith was hit by vigilante fire but maintained his charge. When the battle ended, Smith walked to a friend's cabin and collapsed. He nearly died from the wounds. The incident did win him the nickname "Bear River".

As his first act, Smith enforced a city ordinance in Abilene prohibiting anyone from carrying guns. His first challenges came from "Big Hank" Hawkins and a man known as Wyoming Frank.

Their burly size nor their pistols intimidated the lawman. Smith quickly overpowered, disarmed, and then banished the pair from town without using a weapon other than his bare hands.

After chasing and arresting a pair of Nebraska rustlers, Smith was given a retroactive raise in pay to two-hundred-twenty-five dollars a month.

One time, a cowboy offered his gun to Smith, who simply told him and his friends, "Just check'em with the bartender boys, and pick 'em up when you're ready to leave town." It wasn't Smith's intention to shut the town down. He just wanted to keep it peaceful.

Smith's fist-fighting ability soon spread to cowboys frequenting Abilene. One man almost bit off his own tongue when the lawman hit him with a blow to the jaw.

"Bear River" Tom rode out to arrest two men suspected of murder in November 1870. Before he reached the house where the men were hiding, Smith was felled with a rifle shot. As he lay wounded, they ran out and killed him with an axe.

Pinkerton Detective Charles Siringo

Charles Siringo
(Google Images)

At twenty-two, Charles Siringo joined the search for Billy-the-Kid. He had to give up the chase when he lost all his money gambling.

During a trip to Chicago, Siringo visited a blind phrenologist who "read" the shape of his skull and told him he should be a detective. He joined the Pinkerton Detective Agency where he built an enviable record over twenty-two-years of service.

In one case, Siringo trailed fugitives through deserts and bad weather, lived with moonshiners and disguised himself as a wanted criminal. This was to convince Efie Landusky, a member of the "Hole-in-the-Wall Gang", to tell him where wanted outlaw Harvey Logan hid.

After twenty-two years, Siringo retired from the agency to write about his adventures.

CHAPTER 18

COMMODORE PERRY OWENS

'He dressed in buckskin and bathed once a week'

Commodore Perry Owens got his name by being born on the fortieth anniversary of Commodore Perry's victory over the British on Lake Erie during the War of 1812.

Commodore Perry
Owens: 1853-1919
(Google Images)

The seafaring name hardly influenced the direction that Perry would take in life. He didn't go to sea, he became a cowboy. Owens became proficient as a marksman and an outstanding racer of horses.

At eighteen years of age, Owen worked various jobs as a cowboy for some of the big Texas cow operations. He learned to rope and brand cattle. When he wasn't working, he was generally practicing with his six-shooter and Winchester rifle.

There is a gap in his history for the next couple of years. It is believed he may have become a buffalo hunter, supplying meat to the railroad workers.

He did arrive in Apache County, Arizona in 1881. Owens became an "enforcer" for a cattle rancher. His job was to prevent the Navajos from stealing the white man's cattle.

Owen surprised some Navajo Indians cutting some steers from a herd one day. The Indians saw his long blonde hair and pale complexion and thought he was one of the many half-breeds in the area. They made gestures of friendship and held out a pipe for smoking.

Owens had other ideas. Instead of smoking, he pulled his gun and shot two of the three men, killing them. The third man quickly rode away without the stolen cattle.

He later worked as a guard for Army cavalry horses in Navajo County. The Indians cast covetous eyes on his long blonde locks. After many attempts to kill him and scatter the Army horses, which failed, the Navajos named him the "Iron Man". Some accounts say he single-handedly held off one hundred Navajo warriors at the stage station in Navajo Springs.

Perry Owens dressed in his buckskins and silver-studded chaps.
(Western History Collections)

Navajos regularly tried to steal the horses, but many of them became targets for Perry Owens' Sharps .50 rifle. He is said to have killed fifty Navajos by the time he became Sheriff of Apache County.

If the Indians got away with horses, Owens would raid them right back, often bringing back more horses than he'd lost.

Commodore Perry Owens was appointed Apache County Sheriff in the fall of 1887, with a jurisdiction of more than twenty-one thousand square miles. The townspeople couldn't quite figure him out.

They often snickered at the way he dressed, with his fringed buckskin jacket and silver-studded chaps. He also wore a wide-brimmed felt hat with his long blonde hair flowing from underneath.

Some observers considered his appearance to be "girlish". He also confused many of them with his habit of taking a bath once a week!

Owens found himself confronted with the Pleasant Valley War. This was a local war where the Blevens and Graham factions on one side were duking it out with the Tewksburys.

Mart Blevins had settled on a ranch at the headquarters of Canyon Creek. With him were five sons, Hampton, John, Charles, Sam Houston, and Andy, who changed his name to Andy Cooper after he had gotten into trouble in Llano, Texas.

Settling in the area soon after was Tom and John Graham, natives of Iowa. The Grahams and the Tewksbury boys were good friends at first, but a quarrel developed over stolen cattle and the relationship soured.

When the Tewksburys had the nerve to bring sheep into cattle country, the conflict grew into all-out war.

"Kill all the sheep and every man with them," Andy Cooper urged.

"No, there must be no killing and no destruction of property," the more reasoned Graham said.

"Give them sheep a foothold in the valley and there won't be enough grass left for a grasshopper come spring," Cooper countered. "I'll lead the boys. We'll make a raid that'll end it all, and damned sudden."

Graham told him to stay put, and stared the gun-handy Andy Cooper down, even though Tom Graham was not known for being a gunman.

The Pleasant Valley conflict turned bloody in February. Shots were fired at a Navajo sheepherder. The herdsman fired back and the Hashknife cowboys that had fired the first shot decided to wait for easier pickings.

A few days later, another Navajo sheepherder was found shot dead.

The Hashknife outfit put John Paine, a big ruthless Texan, in charge of moving sheepmen off Hashknife range. Paine and his riders gave ultimatums to the Tewksbury sheepmen. Leave, or else.

Even though things cooled down when the sheep were removed, it had cost Tewksbury brothers a considerable amount of money. They were even more rankled because they had lost the skirmish to the Grahams.

It was well-known that Andy Cooper was a horse thief. It was also known that Sheriff Owens had a warrant for his arrest from a previous occasion. In his efforts to keep calm in the county, Owens let the warrant against Cooper gather dust.

When the horses of Mormon teamsters began disappearing, the tense situation mounted. The editor of the *Apache County Critic* wrote, "The leader of this gang of rustlers has been cited as one Andy Cooper, who was classed as being a horse thief desperado of the most daring stamp, and the boldest man in his operations as had ever cursed the west."

Owens brought in lawbreaker after lawbreaker and collected license fee after license fee, and his reputation grew. However, horses and cattle continued to disappear, and the newspaper hammered for the arrest of Cooper. Owens still held the warrant without serving it.

The situation became tenser when Mart Blevens rode away from his Canyon Creek ranch one morning and didn't return. The Blevins brothers were convinced Mart was killed by the sheepmen.

A group of Hashknife riders, led by John Paine, went to the Middleton ranch where Jim and Ed Tewksbury were now pasturing their sheep. With them were Jim Roberts and Joseph Boyer.

According to Roberts, Hampton Blevins reached for his pistol. Jim Tewksbury, deadly with a saddle gun, shot him dead. Jim Roberts fired at John Paine, clipping his ear and splattering the side of his head with blood. Another Tewksbury bullet felled Paine's horse. As Paine jumped away from the falling animal, he, too, was shot by Tewksbury bullets.

Owens was ordered by the county board of commissioners to either arrest Andy Cooper within ten days or face ouster from office. Days later, more men died. A group of riders descended on John Tewksbury's home and killed the rancher and William Jacobs.

The cowboys kept the remaining Tewksburys pinned down inside the house. Hogs came and rooted at the dead bodies laying in the yard. Finally, Mary Ann Tewksbury could no longer stand it.

She braved the guns of Graham and his riders and dug a shallow grave, where she buried her husband and his Jacobs. The cowboys held their fire while she completed the task.

Andy Cooper bragged about committing the killings. When druggist Frank Wattron asked Owens if he wanted help,

Owens said, "I don't want anyone hurt in this matter. They've been telling all around the country that I was afraid to serve these Cooper warrants, and a lot of other stuff. I'll show them that I'm not afraid and take him single-handed or die a-trying. You just sit back and watch me do it, that's all I ask."

When the Blevins riders, including Andy Cooper got their horses to leave town, Sheriff Owens walked out of the livery stable with his Winchester .45-60 in hand. A few minutes later, Andy Cooper and Sam Houston Blevins were dead and John Blevins was wounded.

Owens did not run for a second term, electing instead to become a guard for the Atlantic & Pacific Railroad. Later he became a Deputy U.S. Marshal under M.K. Meade.

At age fifty, Owens married Elizabeth Barrett, twenty-three-years old. The couple had no children. When he reached his sixties, Owens' mind failed. He died May 10, 1919.

CHAPTER 19

ALLAN PINKERTON

In his native Scotland, Allan Pinkerton was a revolutionary agitator for workingmen's reforms. Threatened with arrest, he and his wife emigrated to the U.S. in 1843.

He settled in Illinois where he helped smuggle runaway slaves to safety in Canada.

Pinkerton's life changed forever when he stumbled across a gang of counterfeiters, and then assisted the police in their capture.

He loved undercover work and joined the Chicago police force as its first detective. He formed his own detective agency in 1850.

Allan Pinkerton
1819-1884
(Pinkerton's, Inc., N.Y.)

Pinkerton hand-picked his detectives. His agency gained nationwide fame for protecting Abraham Lincoln during his campaign at the beginning of his presidency. On Lincoln's orders, Pinkerton created a Secret Service in Washington, D.C., to help weed out Confederate sympathizers and spies. He eventually sent them as undercover agents into camps and cities in the South.

Criminals everywhere feared Pinkerton. They called him the eye, which is depicted in his "logo" here. (Pinkerton's, Inc., New York)

When the Civil War ended, Pinkerton's agency flourished nationwide. He then set his sights on bringing to justice outlaws of the west.

The James boys were wreaking such havoc on the railroads that bankers decided something had to be done. They called on the Pinkerton agency to thwart the outlaw train robbers.

Pinkerton faced blank walls everywhere he went to gather information on the James Gang. Three of Pinkerton's agents were killed in shootouts in a single week soon after the newest train robbery. Two of the agents were killed by John and Jim Younger, two of the four notorious Younger brothers that were a big part of the James gang.

John Younger himself was killed in the shootout. The surviving brothers, Cole, Bob and Jim, took temporary refuge in Dallas, where they sang in a Baptist choir, but made periodic trips north to participate in another robbery.

Pinkerton agents, in 1875, finally were able to get close to the James family's Missouri homestead. One Pinkerton agent posed as a farmhand at the place across the road. On January 26, a force of detectives was brought in by special train.

They surrounded the James house. Their scheme backfired, however, when an agent tossed a round metal object, either a grenade or a flare intended to illuminate the house.

The device exploded and shattered the right arm of Zeralda Samuel, the James boys' mother, and killed her nine-year-old son by her second marriage.

Bob, Jim, Cole and Sister Henrietta Younger, 1889.
(Google Images)

Zeralda let it be known far and wide that her sons, Jesse and Frank, had not even been at home that night. This turned the James boys into martyrs in the public eye.

Pressure from Pinkerton's agents did have an effect on the James gang's activities. They decided to head north, a decision that would find them engaged in one of their biggest shootouts of their lives.

Jesse and Frank James, along with three of the Younger brothers and three other outlaws, rode into the town of Northfield, Minnesota. Three of the gang went in to the First National Bank to make what they thought would be a routine withdrawal.

To their surprise, the rest of the gang came under attack from the town's citizens who armed themselves with rifles and shotguns commandeered from the town's two hardware stores.

Inside the bank, Jesse killed a cashier, then he and his two outlaw companions exited the bank only to find one of their gang was dead and the street was ablaze with gunfire. Another outlaw then fell dead and four more suffered wounds before the gang was able to make its exit.

Allan Pinkerton, seated right, with his agents for the Union Army Secret Service.   (Google Images)

In a space of twenty minutes, the aroused people of Northfield had accomplished what law officials had not been able to do for a decade. They had put the James gang out of commission.

By the early 1890s, Pinkerton   National Detective Agency's two-thousand active agents and thirty-thousand reserves were larger than the standing army of the United States.

The agency's success depended on both armed guards and the clandestine efforts of secret operatives.

For instance James McParlan, infiltrated Irish anthracite miners' organizations in the mid-1870s. McParlan's testimony helped send ten men to the gallows and broke the miners' union for a generation.

Labor leaders despised the Pinkerton agents. Homestead, Minnesota Mayor "Honest" John McLuckie describes this feeling at Andrew Carnegies Homestead Mill.

"Our people think they are a horde of cut-throats, thieves, and murderers and are in the employ of unscrupulous capital for the oppression of honest labor."

In the late nineteenth century, labor disputes often erupted into violent riots. Local sheriffs were usually too poorly equipped or too sympathetic to labor to put down the strikes.

The Pinkerton Detective Agency, on the other hand, staked its reputation on crushing labor actions. Between 1866 and 1892, Pinkertons participated in seventy labor disputes and opposed more than one-hundred-twenty-five-thousand strikers.

William Pinkerton and railroad special agents in late 1870s.
(Google Images)

Whether it influenced his feelings toward organized labor or not, it is important to note that Pinkerton's father, William Pinkerton, was killed during a political riot in Glasgow, Scotland. The Pinkerton family was left fatherless and young Allan Pinkerton left school to work.

Allan and his new bride left Scotland for Canada when he heard that a company of soldiers was on their way to arrest him for his political activities. The ship floundered when it neared Halifax, Canada and finally rammed on a reef.

Pinkerton and his wife lost everything they owned except for the clothes they wore and a few pieces of silver in Allan's vest pocket. When they clambered to shore,

they were immediately set upon by Indians demanding
their trinkets.

When one savage spotted
Mrs. Pinkerton's gleaming
silver wedding band, he
insisted she hand it over. Allan
wanted to fight to keep the
wedding band, but the
practical-minded sea captain
convinced them it was better to
lose the ring than their life.

On board the rescue boat,
Pinkerton decided that he
would settle in the United
States instead of Quebec, his
original destination.

Allan and Joan Pinkerton
later in life.
(Pinkertons, Inc.)

He heard of the marvels of
Chicago that sat on the eastern
fringe of the frontier. Chicago was spreading out and
quickly becoming a city that needed craftsmen of all
kinds.

The Pinkerton Agency was the forerunner of the
Federal Bureau of Investigation (FBI).

Pinkerton became a master at messing with the minds
of his quarry.

In 1856, when a bank teller was murdered in a
bungled hold-up attempt, Pinkerton had a prime suspect
but nothing concrete to pin on the man.

He hired a detective that had a remarkable
resemblance to the dead man, and had him shadow the
suspect. The killer thought he was being hounded by the
ghost of the victim. Eventually he broke down and
confessed to the crime. He then committed suicide.

Allan Pinkerton died July 1, 1884 of an accidental
injury that became infected with gangrene.

Thomas 'Heck" Thomas

Heck Thomas

One of the "Three Guardsmen" that cleared Oklahoma Territory of outlaws, Heck Thomas was considered one of the west's most effective lawmen.

Thomas collected the reward for killing William Doolin. According to one tale that circulated, Thomas actually found Doolin dead of consumption. He then blasted the body with his shotgun before taking the body into the coroner.

Another story is that he gave the reward money to Doolin's widow.

On his first excursion in Indian Territory, he apprehended eight murderers, a bootlegger, a horse thief and seven other outlaws.

Working with the other two Guardsmen, Chris Madsen and Bill Tilghman, the lawmen arrested more than three-hundred wanted men.

CHAPTER 20

JOSEPH LAFAYETTE MEEK

Joe Meek
1810-1875
(Google Images)

Joe Meek went west to get away from a disagreeable stepmother. His later encounters in the west would make his disagreements with his stepmother seem mild, indeed.

His first stop after leaving his Washington County, Virginia home was to Missouri, where he joined two brothers.

He later signed on as a trapper with William Sublette of the Rocky Mountain Fur Company. He lived the strenuous life of a mountain man for the next eleven years.

Meek later told of a "hand-to-paw" encountered with a grizzly bear, a narrow escape in a confrontation with a Blackfoot warrior, the death of his first Indian wife in an attack by a Bannock raiding party, and his second marriage to the daughter of a Nez Percé chief.

Here is one story that Meek gleefully told to any who would listen:

Joe Meek told this story of two mountain men in a confrontation with a bear.   (Google Images)

"The first fall on the Yellowstone, Hawkins and myself were coming up the river in search of camp, when we discovered a very large bar on the opposite bank. We shot across, and thought we had killed him, fur he laid quite still.

"As we wanted to take some trophy of our victory to camp, we tied our mules and left our guns, clothes, and everything except our knives and belts, and swum over to whar the bar war.

"But instead of being dead, as we expected, he sprung up as we come near him, and took after us. Then you ought to have seen two naked men run! It war a race for life, and a close one, too.

"But we made the river first. The bank war about fifteen feet high above the water, and the river ten or twelve feet deep; but we didn't halt. Overboard we went, the bar after us, and in the stream about as quick as we war.

"The current war very strong, and the bar war about half way between Hawkins and me. Hawkins was trying to swim down stream faster than the current war carrying the bar, and I war a trying to hold back.

"You can reckon that I swam! Every moment I felt myself being washed into the yawning jaws of the mighty beast, whose head war up the stream, and his eyes on me. But the current war too strong for him, and swept him along as fast as it did me.

"All this time, not a long one, we war looking for some place to land where the bar could not overtake us. Hawkins war the first to make the shore, unknown to the bar, whose head war still up stream; and he set up such a whooping and yelling that the bar landed too, but on the opposite side.

"I made haste to follow Hawkins, who had landed on the side of the river we started from, either by design or good luck, and then we traveled back a mile and more to whar our mules war left--a bar on one side of the river, and too *bares* on the other! "

In 1863, Meek traveled to California with mountain man Joseph Walker, crossing over the Sierra and into Yosemite Valley. Meek eventually settled in Oregon with his third Indian wife and their family. He became a farmer and an activist in the effort to make Oregon a part of the United States.

He served as sheriff in 1843, under the newly formed provisional government, and then was elected to the legislature in 1846 and 1847. When Congress approved Oregon's territorial status in 1848, President James Polk appointed Meek the territories federal marshal.

Meek's biographer, Stanley Vestal, described Meek as "The Davy Crockett of our Great Northwest." According to

Vestal, Meek was "...the wittiest, saltiest, most shameless wag and jester that ever wore moccasins in the Rockies..."

In his capacity as U.S. Marshal, Meek supervised the hanging of five Cayuse Indians. The Indians were found guilty of the Whitman Massacre, in which an establishment of missionaries was slaughtered.

CHAPTER 21

HENRY BULL HEAD

The Battle with the Ghost Dancers

It was going to be a tough job. Lieutenant Henry Bull Head was charged with the task of arresting his old friend Sitting Bull.

The army believed this was the only way to cool down the "Ghost Dance" craze that permeated through the Indian reservation. The Indians who performed the ritual believed it would free them from oppression by the white man.

A Ghost Dancer
(Google Images)

By the 1880s, the U.S. government confined most all Indians on reservations on land so poor that the white man had no use for it. The rations and supplies guaranteed the Indians were of poor quality if they ever arrived at all.

The poor conditions of the Indians made the situation ripe for a major movement to envelop among them. This movement found its origin in a Paiute Indian named Wovoka, who claimed he was the messiah come to earth to prepare the Indians for their salvation.

An Indian Ghost Dance   (Google Images)

Representatives of Indian tribes from all over the nation came to Nevada to meet with Wovoka and learn to dance the Ghost Dance and to sing Ghost Dance songs.

In October 1890, Kicking Bear, a Minneconjou, visited Sitting Bull at Standing Rock Indian Reservation. He told the Indian chief of his visit to Wovoka, whom he referred to as the Christ. He told of the Ghost Dance he had learned and how the Christ had flown over the Indians on their ride back to the railroad.

He related the prophecy of Wovoka, which said that next spring, when the grass was high, the earth would be covered with new soil, burying all the white men. The new soil would be covered with sweet grass, running water and trees, the great herds of buffalo and wild horses would return.

All Indians who danced the Ghost Dance would be taken up into the air and suspended there while the new earth was being laid down. Then they would be replaced there, with the ghosts of their ancestors, on the new earth. Only Indians would live there then.

Wovaka

This new religion was being taught at all the Sioux reservations. Indian agents were getting nervous about all the dancing and even calling for soldiers to come in on some reservations.

As the number of people involved in the Ghost Dance movement increased, the panic and concern of the Indian agents increased. The messiah doctrine of Wovoka had taken a firm hold upon Sitting Bull and his followers. Sitting Bull apparently believed this new Ghost Dance craze was what he needed to assert himself as "high priest", and regain his popularity and status among the Sioux.

The Indians who believed in the Ghost Dance had given up any industrial pursuits and even abandoned their houses. They had all moved into camp in the immediate neighborhood of Sitting Bull's house. Their entire time was consumed in doing the Ghost Dance and in the vapor bath preparation they conducted before doing the dance.

The only exception was the second Saturday of each month, when they went to the Agency for the meager supplies it doled out.

Major James McLaughlin was the Indian agent at Standing Rock, Dakota. He had been ordered to suppress any threatened outbreaks among the Sioux Indians by force if necessary.

The order for the arrest of Sitting Bull came to Major McLaughlin on December 12, 1890. The arrest was scheduled for December 20. Thwarting the plan was an urgent letter from Lieutenant of Police Henry Bull Head, Indian peace officer in charge of the force on Grand River. Lieutenant Bull Head said that Sitting Bull was preparing to leave the reservation.

Sitting Bull had fitted his horses for a long and hard ride, Policeman Henry Bull Head informed McLaughlin. If Sitting Bull, being so well-mounted, got a head start, it would be difficult for the police to overtake him.

It was decided that the police should make the arrest of Sitting Bull at the break of day the following morning.

Lieutenant Henry Bull Head was a friend of Sitting Bull. "I was with him when he led our people across the border and into the Grandmother's country. I did not return to the United States and surrender my rifle until he did.," he told Agent McLaughlin. "

"I know about your friendship, Henry, " McLaughlin informed him. "That is why I'm charging you with the job of arresting him. General Miles (Nelson A. Miles) agrees that the only way to take the steam out of this Ghost Dance craze is to remove Sitting Bull from Grand River."

Lieutenant Bull Head led thirty-nine reservation policemen and four volunteers, one of which was Sitting Bull's brother-in-law, "Gray Eagle", into Sitting Bull's camp at daybreak on December 16, 1890.

They proceeded directly to Sitting Bull's house. When Lt. Bull Head entered Sitting Bull's house, the chief was asleep. Upon awakening, he agreed to accompany Lieutenant Bull Head and asked that his horse be saddled while he dressed.

It was then that Sitting Bull's son, Crow Foot, who was also in the house, began berating his father for accepting the arrest and agreeing to go with the police. Changing his mind, Sitting Bull then became stubborn as well.

When the police took Sitting Bull outside, they were soon surrounded by his Ghost Dance followers that far outnumbered the police force. Lt. Bull Head reasoned with them, gradually expanding the circle surrounding Sitting Bull. Lieutenant Bullhead and two sergeants guarded the chief.

Sitting Bull called on his followers to immediately kill Bull Head and Shave Head, the two principal policemen. "Kill these two men and the others will run away," he cried.

One Ghost Dancer, Catch-the-Bear, dashed into the crowd with a rifle and fired. The shot struck Lieutenant Bull Head in the side, causing the lieutenant to turn. As he turned, his gun accidentally fired, shooting Sitting Bull in the side between the tenth and eleventh ribs.

The Indian whose shot hit Lieutenant Bull Head was immediately shot down by a member of the arresting party. The fight then became a hand-to-hand conflict between forty-three policemen and volunteers against about one-hundred-fifty crazed Ghost Dancers.

"I cannot too strongly commend the splendid courage and ability which characterized the conduct of the Indian police commanded by Bull Head and Shave Head throughout the encounter," McLaughlin wrote in a report.

McLaughlin concluded his report by saying, "After the fight, no demoralization seemed to exist among them, (the Indians) and they were ready and willing to cooperate with the troops to any extent desired."

Henry Bull Head died eighty-two hours after the fight. So did fourteen others. Four others were wounded.

CHAPTER 22

HENRY NEWTON BROWN

Henry Brown seemingly had a clean slate based on what he told the city council in Caldwell, Kansas when they hired him as assistant marshal in 1882. It's what he didn't tell them which was more interesting.

By age eighteen, like many other young men his age, he turned to buffalo hunting in Texas. Under mysterious circumstances that never became known, Brown killed a man in Texas.

This didn't stop him from getting a job as assistant marshal at Caldwell and being appointed marshal at the end of the year.

Henry Brown
1857-1884

Caldwell was about as wild and wooly as a town can get.

Brown arrived on the job at Caldwell as the city recorded four murders (all of them lawmen) and eight lynchings. If *The Caldwell Post* was right, Henry Brown was well-equipped to handle the job. The paper exclaimed the he was "one of of the quickest men on the trigger in the Southwest."

What the townsfolk didn't realize, was that Brown picked up his quick gunplay on the wrong side of the law.

He had ridden with Billy the Kid, been involved in stealing horses, and fled from New Mexico to avoid murder charges.

Brown took his assistant marshal's job seriously. He was quiet and businesslike, and so popular the city council promoted him to the full marshal's job after only six months.

The city fathers liked Henry Brown's performance so well that on New Year's Day 1883, they presented him with a spanking new Winchester rifle.

There were few if any complaints when Henry killed two miscreants in the line of duty. *The Caldwell Commercial* newspaper lauded him as "...cool, courageous and gentlemanly, and free from...vices."

Henry married Alice Levagood, a local girl, in 1884. The couple purchased a house and seemed to settle down. Brown, however, was living beyond his means and debts played heavily on his mind.

In order to cover his debts, Brown fell back on his old ways. He devised a plan that included his assistant marshal, Ben Wheeler, and two cowboys, John Wesley and Billy Smith.

The four men hitched their horses behind the coal shed of the Medicine Valley Bank. The bank had just opened. Three of the men burst through the door while the fourth waited outside.

The bank president reached for his gun. Brown shot him. The clerk was shot twice by another of the robbers and died soon after.

John Wesley, Henry Brown, Billy Smith, and Ben
Wheeler are shackled after their failed attempt to rob
the Medicine Lodge Bank.   (Google Images)

An eager posse chased the robbers as they fled town.
The bandits surrendered after being trapped in a box
canyon outside of town.

"Hang them!" a hungry mob chanted outside the
Medicine Lodge Jail. Brown apparently realized his days
were short. He drafted a letter to his wife of six weeks. "I
will send you all of my things, and you can sell them, but
keep the Winchester."

That night the angry mob broke into the jail to take
the prisoners. The prisoners made a dash for freedom.
Henry Brown fell dead, riddled with buckshot and balls
from the mob's rifles.

Brown's widow continued to live in Caldwell after his
death, but ignored his instructions about the Winchester.
She gave the rifle to friends, who later sold or gave it to
someone in Texas. Two generations later, the rifle was
sold to a gun collector. It was donated to the Kansas
Museum of History.

CHAPTER 23

SAM GAY

'The Lovable Lawman'

Sam Gay
1860-1932
(Google Images)

On a typical day in Clark County, Nevada, Sheriff Sam Gay busted up a hobo camp outside of town, where he nabbed a couple of muggers, who were identified and arrested.

Gay found a cache of stolen goods and money. While at it, he nabbed a convict who had fled the Idaho State Prison.

If those duties weren't enough, Gay also dealt with the theft of a furnished house. It was just a tent house on a wooden foundation, but it was gone and was never recovered. This may have been one of his better days.

"Big Sam Gay" was muscular and weighed two-hundred-sixty pounds. He was touted as the toughest lawman in town, although he wore no gun while keeping the peace.

Sam Gay moved to Las Vegas in 1905 where he worked first as a night watchman. It wasn't long before he became chief deputy for Sheriff Charles Corkhill. In 1910, he ran against Sheriff Corkhill and defeated him.

Gay later became Police Chief of Las Vegas. When confronted by rowdies, Gay didn't hesitate to tie them to a hitching post and "hose" them down through the night. At the same time, he was known as a compassionate man who was never known to abuse his authority or mistreat prisoners.

When criticism was leveled at him, it was more often for being too lax or lenient. He believed that the men who toiled in the mines or drove freight wagons were entitled to get drunk, gamble and raise hell.

It was Gay's job to keep them from killing, robbing or seriously wounding each other.

Sheriff Gay was born on Prince Edward Island, Canada on March 1, 1860. He grew up on a stock and dairy farm. He moved to North Dakota where he was in charge of a wheat farm. He then worked as a motorman and conductor on the San Diego Electric Railroad.

His first job in law enforcement was as city marshal in the city of Coronado, California. Lured by gold being found in Nevada, he went to Goldfield to work in the deep mines.

Tex Rickard, owner of the Northern Club in Goldfield, then hired Gay as a bouncer. In 1905, at age forty-five, Gay took a job as a bouncer in Las Vegas at J.O. McIntosh's Arizona Club.

When Orrin K. Smith was elected sheriff of Lincoln County in 1908, he hired Sam Gay as his deputy for the southern part of the big county. His job was to keep peace in the rowdy Block 16, where he was faced with barroom brawls.

When Lincoln County split, creating Clark County, Charles C. Corkhill was elected sheriff. Corkhill was the editor of *The Las Vegas Age,* and he believed in running the sheriff's department "by the book." Gay, on the other hand, relied on his own judgment and experience.

The Las Vegas jail was a large, windowless shack, made of sheet metal and railroad ties. In the summer of 1910, Sam Gay opened the doors to the airless, rat-infested jail.

He chained the prisoners together and marched them to the old Las Vegas Ranch. There, he tied them loosely to the giant cottonwoods along Las Vegas Creek where they could stay cool.

This infuriated Sheriff Corkhill and he fired Deputy Gay. This turned out to be a mistake for Corkhill. Sam Gay challenged him at the polls and won.

While he did not normally draw his weapon on duty, Gay did enjoy sports shooting. One of his favorite sports was to get quite drunk and shoot out electric lights. One night, he got quite drunk and began shooting the lights out on Fremont Street. District Attorney Albert Henderson charged him with gross intoxication.

When Gay appeared in court, he did not admit guilt nor defend himself. Instead, he told the court, "So long as I am sheriff of Clark County, I will not take a drink of intoxicating liquor. If I do, I will hand in my resignation." The court dropped the charges.

He later said that Prohibition helped him keep his temperance pledge. "I quit after they started making the stuff out of old shoes. They call it good whiskey and make faces when drinking it. When I did my drinking, men smacked their lips as it rolled down."

About a month after he took his dramatic courtroom pledge, a small girl named Marjorie Schaeffer met him on the street. She handed him a small box marked "Sheriff Sam". When he opened it, he found a heavy solid gold badge with the words, "Sheriff, Clark County, Nevada on its face. An inscription said, "Compliments of Las Vegas Friends."

Gay was moved by the gift and told *The Las Vegas Age* that he would keep the badge "bright and unsullied".

From the time Sam was charged with "gross intoxication", a rift existed between Gay and District Attorney Henderson.

The rift widened over the wide-open gambling that took place in Las Vegas even though gambling had been outlawed since 1910. District Attorney Henderson charged Sheriff Gay's deputy, Joe Keate, with not only allowing a poker game to take place at the Northern Club, but of participating in it as well.

It was an election year, so Sheriff Gay duly fired Deputy Keate—but only for one day.

Deputy Keate was a hothead that caused a lot of his own trouble. In one incident, Keate was ordered to fetch a prisoner from jail and bring him to the courtroom. Because the order came from Justice of the Peace William Harkins instead of his boss, Keate took his time, dawdling along Fremont Street.

When he did arrive at the court, an hour late, Harkins fined him five dollars for contempt of court. Keate refused to pay. Instead, he rushed from the court, borrowed a gun, returned to court and placed the borrowed gun in front of Harkins, demanding a fight.

Sheriff Gay heard the rumor and went in the courtroom just in time to see the drama, with Keate poised with his hand over his holster, ready to draw.

Harkins demanded that Gay arrest the deputy, but the sheriff refused. He waited until his deputy had cooled down and then led him away.

Sheriff Gay was fired for failing to discharge his duties. He fought back in court, asserting that as an elected official, he could not be fired. The case went to the Nevada Supreme Court, which upheld the firing.

When he sought re-election in 1918, he easily won. Sam won re-election again in 1926. He then felt he was getting too old for the job.

"Too many crooks coming to Las Vegas, now they're building Boulder Dam," he said. "I've dealt with honest men so long, I wouldn't know how to act around crooks. I'm used to tough hombres who shoot each other up once in a while.

"I'm used to gunfights. But I ain't much good running down racketeers. My notions are too old-fashioned. You can't deal with these new gunmen with a single-action .45. Need a machine gun. I'm too old to learn to run one, so I quit."

(Author's note: Much of the information for this chapter on Sheriff Sam Gay came from an article by K.J. Evans and published in the *Las Vegas Review-Journal*.)

CHAPTER 24

BIG DAVE UPDIKE

'He wouldn't tell where they hid the gold'

A crooked sheriff was an accomplice in this stage holdup.
(Google Images)

David Updyke saved about fifteen-hundred-dollars working a pretty good claim on Ophir Mountain in Idaho. He took his money to Boise City and bought a livery stable in the center of town.

The livery stable soon became the rendezvous site for some of the most reckless bands of robbers and road agents around. This, however, did not keep Updyke from being elected Sheriff of Ada County.

Soon after his election, Updyke vowed he would break up the Payette River Vigilance Committee. This put him on the wrong side of the law-abiding citizens who felt the vigilance committee was their only protection from thieving and murdering road agents taking over the area.

Updyke obtained the names of all the men in the vigilante group and procured warrants for their arrest. Updyke and his "posse" secretly planned to shoot the vigilante leaders and maintain they had resisted arrest.

One night in 1865, four outlaws met in a Boise City, Idaho saloon to plan the robbery of the stage that barreled through Idaho Territory along a route going from Montana to Utah.

The leader of the outlaw group was Brockie Jack, who busted out of jail in Oregon. Others in the group included livery stable owner and sheriff David Updyke, Willy Whitmore, a gunman with a hot temper and a man named Fred Williams.

According to plan, Williams was sent to Virginia City, Montana to gain information on the gold shipments. Stagecoaches on the Portneuf Road between Virginia City, Montana and Pocatello, Idaho often carried gold from the Montana mines.

Once he was sure the stagecoach would carry the gold cargo, Williams would buy a ticket and ride along as a passenger. The other three bandits, meanwhile, traveled south along the stage route looking for a perfect holdup site.

They chose a site just south of present-day Pocatello. It was a narrow and rocky canyon that was heavily timbered and filled with brush. The site seemed perfect. The outlaws then gathered enough boulders to block the stage road. These were hid from sight until needed later.

The plan called for Willy Whitmore, with his Henry repeating rifle, to shoot the lead horses if the stage driver should try to go around the boulders. With the plan in place, the three bandits returned to Ross Fork Creek to wait for Fred Williams and the stagecoach.

154

It was nearly two weeks later when the stagecoach left Virginia City. Charlie Parks was the driver, and the stage carried seven passengers, including the outlaw, Fred Williams.

For the next three days, the stagecoach traveled along Union Pacific Railroad tracks towards Pocatello. On the fourth night, the stage stopped at Sodhouse Station to spend the night.

After the evening meal, Williams excused himself and headed to Ross Fork Camp where his cohorts were waiting. They were ecstatic to hear the news of the two strongboxes. Williams returned to Sodhouse Station. No one noticed he had been gone.

The next day, the stagecoach reached the stream near where the outlaws planned to rob it. The stage slowed to cross the stream. As it traveled up the far bank, it suddenly stopped. The road was blocked by the boulders the bandits had secreted earlier.

The three bandits then appeared with guns drawn. One passenger, a gambler named Sam Martin, drew his own gun. He aimed it at Whitmore. The shot tore off the left index finger of Whitmore.

"It's a trap," Whitmore shouted, and he began emptying his gun into the side of the stagecoach. When driver Charlie Parks tried to break through the brush with the team and stagecoach, Brockie Jack shot both lead horses, stopping the stage dead in its tracks.

Parks, the driver, jumped from the stage and dashed for the nearby woods. Both Fred Williams, the outlaw accomplice, and a passenger named James B. Brown, a Virginia City saloon keeper, also ran for the woods.

Brockie Jack grabbed the rifle from Whitmore and approached the stagecoach while Whitmore and Updyke covered him. When he opened the door, he found the remaining passengers inside seemed to be dead. The exception was a man named L.F. Carpenter, who feigned death in order to survive.

Fred Williams staggered from the woods with a shattered arm. The three outlaws were so busy looting the stagecoach and its passengers they scarcely noticed Williams' plight.

When Whitmore and Brockie Jack smashed the two strong boxes open with an ax, they discovered fifteen gold bars and two pouches filled with gold dust and nuggets. The four outlaws packed up and rode out of the canyon.

Driver Charlie Parks and James B. Brown emerged from the woods. Brown pulled the still-breathing Carpenter from under the dead bodies and made him and the injured Parks as comfortable as he could.

Brown then cut the stage loose from the two dead lead horses and the group drove on to Miller Ranch Station.

There, the survivors told their stories. Parks recognized both Brockie Jack and David Updyke, while James Brown positively identified Fred Williams and Willy Whitmore.

A ten-thousand-dollar reward was posted by the insurance company for information leading to the recovery of the eighty-five-thousand-dollars in gold.

A vigilance committee issued orders for the criminals to be hung once captured.

First to be captured was the hot-tempered Willy Whitmore. He was found while on a drinking binge in Arizona. When he resisted arrest, he was shot. Fred Williams was captured in Colorado and hung by a vigilance committee there. Both men were penniless when they were killed.

The vigilantes were more cautious when it came to dealing with David Updyke, the duly elected Sheriff of Ada County. The Payette River Vigilance Committee arrested Updyke on a charge of defrauding the revenue of

Ada County, and for failing to arrest a hard case criminal named West Jenkins.

Updyke was able to make bail, but knowing the reputation of the Vigilance Committee, he quickly left town, fleeing to Boise City where he felt he held more influence.

He was wrong. The citizens there were also fed up with the criminal element and began to form groups for the purpose of cleaning up the county. Updyke feared for his own safety. He joined another outlaw, John Dixon, and departed Boise.

A vigilante party, unknown by the two outlaws, followed them. They were captured thirty miles out of town in an abandoned cabin.

When Updyke was questioned about the whereabouts of the stolen gold, he glared at them in contempt, refusing to respond. The vigilantes then hung both men. Updyke had only fifty-dollars on him at the time of his death.

The fourth outlaw, Brockie Jack just disappeared. There is no record of the gold ever being found.

The Wild Bunch

Butch Cassidy and his Wild Bunch gang.
(Google Images)

In 1901, Butch Cassidy and The Sundance Kid were hunted by a hand-picked posse, consisting of lawmen and agents from Pinkerton's Detective Agency.

The Wild Bunch used the "Hole-in-the-Wall" as their hideout, frustrating law enforcement officials. This area was located where the state lines of Utah, Colorado and Wyoming now meet.

The Hole-in-the-Wall was a near impenetrable fortress of towering cliffs, deep gorges and mountainous hideouts.

Cassidy and The Sundance Kid fled to Argentina where The Sundance Kid shot a rancher. They were declared outlaws and had to flee to Bolivia. Since they were now declared outlaws, they took up outlawry seriously. They became known as the *Banditos Yankee.*

It is believed they were killed in Bolivia by soldiers who discovered their identities.

CHAPTER 25

THE LOS ANGELES RANGERS

'Their reign was short-lived'

Organized bands of outlaws infested Los Angeles in the 1850s. There was little if any law and order.

The Los Angeles Rangers provided a posse to help the understaffed Sheriff's Department.
(Google Images)

More than one-hundred-thousand men from every quarter of the globe were thrown together in a new land without an established government.

In an effort to protect the citizens of Los Angeles from frequent raids by these outlaws, a volunteer militia group that became known as "The Los Angeles Rangers" was organized in 1853. It was under the command of Captain A.W. Hope.

Severe verdicts were the rule in early-day California. For example, for stealing read, "...should in one hour be hung by the neck until dead."

Another common punishment was whipping on the bare back of the convicted. Sometimes culprits were branded on the cheek with the letter "R" (renegade). Their hair and eyebrows were frequently shaved.

A jury was composed of eight American citizens unless the accused desired a jury of twelve. The jurors would be summoned by the sheriff and sworn by the *Alcalde,* and "shall try the case according to the evidence."

The first Sheriff's Department of Los Angeles was formed in 1850. It called for the re-election of the sheriff annually. In 1882, the term was increased to two years. The first sheriff in the county was George T. Burrill. His staff consisted of two deputies.

Because of this shortage of manpower, The Los Angeles Rangers were formed in 1852. The rangers provided a posse, ready to ride, and were under the direction of the Sheriff's office. The Rangers wore a white ribbon, which said in both English and Spanish, "City Police—Authorized by the Council of Los Angeles.

The L.A. Rangers had sixty active members, and crimes did decrease. The Rangers attended the first judicial execution of persons arrested by them in Los Angeles on February 22, 1854.

When the first Los Angeles Rangers condemned man, a Mexican named Herrera, came before the court, he was convicted of murder. On the same docket were three other men and a woman on charges of robbery and murder. The prisoners were all convicted, placed in jail and almost immediately all escaped.

Again the aid of the Rangers was enlisted. The escapees were recaptured and held in the custody of soldiers for safe-keeping until time for their execution.

The Los Angeles Rangers were replaced by the Los Angeles City Guards which were organized in 1855. The unit was still in existence in 1861, but few historical records show any of the guards' later activities and it is assumed the unit was abandoned that year.

Lynch law struck terror into the hearts of many criminals in California. There was simply no undefined view of a convicted felon's ultimate fate under such law. Vigilante committees in other parts of California encouraged hard-bitten criminals to move south.

Many of them congregated in Los Angeles County, which at that time included present-day counties of Kern, Orange, San Bernardino and Ventura. Los Angeles boasted of more murders annually, in proportion to population, than any other community in California.

Los Angeles' first paid police force was not created until 1869 when a force of six officers under City Marshal William C. Warren were hired.

The new city marshal and his staff had less than a happy relationship. Warren was shot by one of his own marshals in 1876.

Calamity Jane

Calamity Jane
(Google Images)

Martha Jane Canary was born in 1852 in Missouri. She became widely-known as Calamity Jane, perhaps the most publicized women of the Old West.

She claimed, after he had been murdered, that Wild Bill Hickok was the father of her child and that they had been married. The child, if it existed, was said to be given up for adoption.

Calamity was little more than a camp follower of gunmen. She was a one-time bordello tart, and in later years, a hopeless alcoholic.

Jane was married to a William Burke in 1891 after they had lived together for at least six years.

She appeared in Wild West shows around the country showing off her shooting and riding skills. She eventually retired to Deadwood where she died of pneumonia in 1903.

CHAPTER 26

FRANK H. DEPENDENER

He was called "Big Dip". because of his height. Indeed he was a big man, standing six-feet-seven-inches tall and of heavy build.

Frank H. Dependener was born in the Rock Creek area north of Auburn, California in 1869. According to information provided by the Placer County Historical Society, Dependener was only twenty-one-years-of-age when he was hired as a jailor by then sheriff William Conroy.

Big Dip found himself in some real trouble when he became involved in a shootout with the Cox brothers in the shadow of the Placer County Courthouse in 1916. Jim and Albert Cox were no strangers to law enforcement officers.

The brothers confronted Deputy Sheriff Dependener when they appeared at the courthouse to post ten dollars in bail for their brother Arthur Cox. The sheriff had arrested Arthur for a minor offense and took him to jail.

When Big Dip turned and walked toward the steps of the Courthouse, without warning, the Cox brothers began firing. The deputy was knocked to his knees and seriously wounded on his gun hand. He was still able to fire by switching his gun to his left hand, and hit one of the Coxes in the arm.

Another bullet from one of the Cox brothers' gun struck Big Dip in the liver. He carried the bullet for two months before it was discovered in an x-ray in Sacramento.

When he was hospitalized, there was no bed long enough for his huge frame. The problem was solved by bringing his own bed from home to the hospital. When word of his injury was spread, well-wishing telegrams came in from all law enforcement groups all over the state.

Big Dip and Shorty Nunes
(Carpo Vino History Archive)

The Cox brothers attack had only heightened his legendary status.

Some newspaper accounts claimed Dependener had been shot at as many as thirty times during his career, but none brought him closer to death than did the shootout with the Cox brothers.

The two brothers fled while they continued to fire aimlessly in the direction of bystanders. They were later arrested and convicted of attempted murder of a peace officer.

In another encounter with Placer county outlaws, Big Dip and Sheriff Conroy were chasing two stage robbers on the North Fork of the American River. The lawmen were then ambushed by the bandits.

Dependener was an excellent marksman. He stood in the open and returned the shots of the outlaws. He was not hit.

Big Dip was called a "lawman's lawman," and was known throughout California and Nevada as being fearless but cool during emergency situations.

To many a fugitive's regret, Dependener never forgot what any outlaw looked like. He would doggedly pursue him until he finally had handcuffs on him.

He told one humorous story on himself. He trailed a man at Lake Tahoe that he thought was a suspect in a crime. He later learned the man was a Hollywood movie actor doing a scene in the public sector.

Big Dip was assigned to collect evidence in one of Auburn's most heinous crimes. At seven-thirty one evening, 1904, a fire raged through the house of Julius Weber, a wealthy Auburn businessman. Fireman found the bodies of Weber, his wife and two of their three children in the ashes after the fire was extinguished.

Julius, his wife and daughter had been shot to death and his youngest son had been beaten and died shortly after being rescued. The bodies had been burned in an attempt to mask the crime.

Weber's twenty-year-old son, Adolph, the only surviving member of the family, was arrested. He was connected to the robbery of the Placer County Bank in Auburn some five months earlier.

Big Dip rode shotgun on the carriage used to transport Adolph to Folsom State Prison where he was sentenced to be hung.

The Placer County Bank in Auburn which Adolph Weber robbed before killing the other members of his family.

(Carpe Vino History Archive)

His daughter, Mignon Young, wife of the late Auburn Police Chief Herschel Young, said her father never wanted to be sheriff, although many Placer County citizens wanted him to be.

She recalled that her father would take her to church on Sundays and then she would meet him at the old Auburn jail afterwards.

In a *San Francisco Chronicle* article, Dependener was featured as the "tallest man in Placer County".

In his book, "Gold and Schemes...and Unfulfilled Dreams," author Bill G. Wilson noted that during prohibition period, Big Dip did not hesitate to quaff a beer with a friend. He was a ferocious opponent, however, of anyone illegally selling alcohol.

It was his dedicated enforcement against the selling of illegal alcohol that resulted in Big Dip's death.

Big Dip was with his boss, Sheriff Elmer Gum, Federal Agent Wallace Polson and a prisoner in the sheriff's Reo Sedan. The three lawmen had just found an illegal still near Roseville. They lashed the barrels of "jackass" whiskey to the sheriff's car to be used as evidence.

The car overturned on a back road a short distance from Auburn. Big Dip, who had never learned to drive, died almost instantly from a broken neck.

His work was highly praised. Sacramento under-sheriff Ellis Jones called him "...one of the best deputies in the country."

Another of Big Dip's daughters, Bea Pavlin, of Auburn, claimed her father "...was the kind of man who would give a crook an even break if the man promised to go straight."

The big lawman spent thirty-seven years with the Auburn sheriff's department.

'Corn Likker'

"Corn Likker" is described thusly:

It smells like gangrene starting in a mildewed silo, it tastes like the wrath to come, and when you absorb a deep swig of it you have all the sensations of having swallowed a kerosene lamp"

Converting surplus corn into whiskey was the most practical way for homesteaders in the remote hills of Kentucky and Tennessee to get their grain to market.

Shipping corn overland was expensive. A packhorse could carry only four bushels of grain across the country, but the same animal could carry the equivalent of twenty-four-bushels of grain when it was condensed into two kegs of whiskey.

Corn whiskey brewers concocted a mashy liquid called still beer. In homemade wooden tubs. they then scalded cornmeal, added barley malt, bran and yeast, and poured in a measure of pure spring water. After letting the mash ferment, they obtained a brew of about seven percent alcohol.

When distilled through a spiral of metal tubing, the alcohol content was increased. The spent "stillage" was saved for hog feed.

CHAPTER 27

HARRY MORSE

He captured Black Bart

Harry Morse gained the reputation of being a persistent and clever man hunter after his election to the sheriff's office for Alameda County, California.

Morse confronted the notorious East Bay thug Narato Ponce, a Chileno, in a real gun battle on Pinole Creek in Contra Costa County in 1867.

Narato was wanted for both murder and horse-stealing.

Even though the outlaw was seemingly shot to pieces by the sheriff, he still fled on foot into the Black Hills of Contra Costa. He was bleeding from thirteen

Harry Morse
1835-1912
(Alameda County
Historical Society)

buckshot and three pistol balls. Governor Frederick Low placed a five-hundred-dollar reward on Ponce's head.

Contra Costa County Sheriff Henry Classen assigned Deputy George Swain to assist Morse in running down the outlaw.

169

The two lawmen found an old man in the Black Hills who had tended the wounds of Ponce. They learned, too, that Ponce was hiding somewhere near Pinole on San Pablo Bay near Vallejo.

Systematically, the lawmen searched the scattered adobes dotting Pinole Valley. When they came to the *jacal* of Jose Rojas, Deputy Swain spotted a man half-buried in the adobe floor underneath the bed.

He also saw the glint of a pistol barrel in the hands of the man. Swain backed out the door, drawing his own weapon at the same time. Swain fired and missed. Oakland police officer John Conway, accompanying Morse and Swain, fired his Henry rifle and also missed.

Ponce ran up the canyon. Sheriff Morse was on the opposite side of the swollen Pinole Creek when he saw the outlaw. He fired his Henry rifle three times and missed because of Ponce's flapping serape.

Officer Conway now had a bead on Ponce. A bullet found its mark, striking the outlaw's right hand.

Ponce was cornered. He stepped to the edge of the creek and took careful aim at Morse. The sheriff fire first, however, and the desperado fell face-down into the mud. He died within five minutes. A coroner's jury of four Anglos and two Hispanics ruled the shooting was justified.

One of the most feared outlaws on the west coast was Juan Soto, also called *The Human Wildcat*. Soto was of mixed Indian and Mexican heritage. He was wanted by California lawmen both for murder and as a thief.

Soto and two other outlaws robbed a store in Sunol, California in 1871. They killed the store clerk and shot several rounds into the quarters of the store owners.

Morse and a deputy followed the outlaws into the Sausalito Valley about fifty miles outside the town of Gilroy. They located Soto and about a dozen of his followers in a make-shift hideout.

When Sheriff Morse told Soto he was under arrest, the outlaw drew a gun. There was a skirmish and Soto fled with Morse right behind him. Soto attempted to mount one of the horses outside the hut. The animal spooked and ran away without Soto.

As Soto ran away, Morse drew a careful bead and nailed him with a single shot. The bullet struck the "Human Wildcat" in the head. He died immediately.

Juan Soto
The Human Wildcat
(California State Library)

Henry Morse's most famous capture would have to be that of "Black Bart", the stagecoach robber that confounded Wells Fargo agents for years.

Black Bart's method of operation was different from other bandits of the day. Bart was no ordinary ruffian. He planned and executed his robberies with careful research and undeniable finesse.

Bart's legend begins at a desolate spot in Calaveras County along the Sonora-Milton stage run. The stage was nearing the top of Funk Hill at the head of Yaqui Gulch. The date was August 3, 1877.

There, a lone highwayman, wearing a long white duster and a flour sack over his head, stepped out in front of a stagecoach. He pointed a double-barreled shotgun at the stage driver.

In a terse, four-word instruction, the bandit ordered: "Please throw down the box."

It was while robbing a stagecoach on the Point Arena-Duncan Mills route that the robber first got the pseudonym Black Bart.

171

The bandit worked alone and left few clues for lawmen to follow. In the box thrown down to the robber was about $300 in coins and a check for $305.52. The check was never cashed. The box was later found empty, except for a bit of poetic doggerel.

The poem read:

I've labored long and hard for bread—
For honor or for riches—
But on my corns too long you've tred,
You fine-haired sons of bitches.

It was signed "**Black Bart, the Po8.**"

While Black Bart's bit of poetic tomfoolery and clean getaway may have caused howls of delight to those who read about the event, rest assured that Wells Fargo officials were not amused.

Black Bart

Wells Fargo offices up and down California were put on lookout for this robber-poet.

In his robberies, he wore a unique mask. Over his head, he wore a flour sack with eyeholes cut in it, atop of which was perched a derby hat. Over what appeared to be rough miners clothing, he wore a soiled linen duster. He covered his boots with heavy woolen socks, apparently to distort his footprints.

"Please throw down the box," Bart would order the driver. While he collected all the loot from the strong boxes, Black Bart never bothered to take the valuables of the passengers.

When one panicked lady tossed him her purse, Black Bart handed it back to her with the reply, "Thank you madam, but I don't need your money. I only want Wells Fargo's."

While he robbed, Black Bart didn't rob frequently. There was often as much as nine months or even a year between holdups. He later told lawmen he "took only what was needed when it was needed."

Black Bart was credited by lawmen with stopping 28 stages over an eight-year period.

To say the least, the bandit had local sheriffs, Wells Fargo detectives and U.S. Postal authorities in a fiery rage. He always stopped the stagecoaches while they were traveling along mountainous roads where the driver was compelled to slow down at dangerous curves.

On November 3, 1883, the Sonora stage was rolling along toward Copperopolis, carrying a lone passenger. The passenger was a young boy with a rifle, who told the driver he wanted to do some hunting. He asked the driver to pick him up on the other side of the hill.

When the boy disappeared, Black Bart appeared, and confronted the stage driver, giving his usual order, "Please throw down the box." Wells Fargo had adopted a new tactic. The company began chaining the box to the floor of the stagecoaches.

Bart ordered the driver to take the horses up over a hill while he worked on the box. While it took the highwayman longer than usual to open the box, he did get it loose by pounding it furiously with his hatchet. He pulled out a knife, slashed the sacks, and extracted the registered letters before telling the driver to move on. The opened letters were found the next day in a nearby ravine.

As the driver was doing so, he met the boy with the rifle coming round the hill. The two hurried back as Black Bart was scrambling into the brush with the loot. The boy sent three shots at the outlaw, wounding him in the hand.

Bart used a handkerchief to wrap his wound. Lawmen later found the bloodied handkerchief, which had a San Francisco laundry mark on it. One of the detectives assigned to track down Black Bart was Henry Nicholson Morse, one-time sheriff of Alameda County. Morse now had his own private detective agency in San Francisco.

Morse faced an arduous task. He had the robber's handkerchief with the laundry mark, FX07, but he soon learned there were ninety-one laundries in San Francisco. He was determined to visit every one of them if necessary.

At Ferguson and Bigg's California Laundry, Morse struck pay dirt. He found the laundry mark belonged to Charles E. Bolton, a mining engineer. Morse arrested Bolton in his hotel room, but when booked, Bolton gave his name as T.Z. Spaulding

In the hotel room, detectives found a Bible that had been given to a Charles E. Boles by his wife in 1865. Born and raised in upper New York State, Boles had been a farmer, and later served as a sergeant in the 116th Illinois Volunteer Infantry just before the Civil War. The lawmen's investigation left them assured that it was Boles who was the much wanted Black Bart.

Records show that Black Bart (Boles) had invested his loot in several small business ventures that provided him a modest income. As money would become short, however, he would return to stagecoach holdups.

Black Bart was convicted January 21, 1988. He was sentenced to six years in San Quentin. This was shortened to four years for good behavior. By the time of his release, he was aging considerably, with both his eyesight and his hearing beginning to fail.

174

As he left the prison, his spirit seemed crushed. He hurried to escape the newsmen that surrounded him when he stepped from the prison gates.

Boles, alias Black Bart, disappeared after his release and was never heard from again.

Black Bart was reported in New York newspapers to have died in 1917, something that was never confirmed. Before that, Detective James B. Hume had received a report that the outlaw had died in the high California mountains while hunting game.

While the outlaw had gained considerable fame for his stage holdups, it should be remembered, he never fired a shot.

The Winchester Rifle

Oliver Winchester established himself in the firearms business in 1857 when he purchased the Volcanic Repeating Arms Company.

He employed Benjamin Tyler Henry as his main gun mechanic. The following year Henry devised a new rifle with a 15 cartridge magazine. The gun was operated by moving the trigger lever down and back to its original position.

This extracted the spent cartridge, carried a fresh shell from the spring-activated tubular magazine into the chamber, and cocked the hammer ready for firing.

The rifle sold well and in 1866 the Winchester Repeating Arms Company was established at New Haven, Connecticut. Soon afterwards an improved version of Benjamin Tyler Henry's rifle was produced.

It was however the 1873 model that was the most successful Winchester. Over the next 40 years the company sold 720,610 of these rifles.

CHAPTER 28

BURTON ALVORD

Working as a stable hand at the O.K Corral, Burt Alvord witnessed one of the most spectacular gunfights of the old west. He was fifteen years old and very impressionable.

The bullet-spitting showdown between the Earp-Holliday clan and the Clanton-McLowery outlaws was an event that stuck in young Burt's mind forever. He had paid close attention to the cool composure of the Earps as they bested the outlaw group.

Burt Alvord
1866-1910

Alvord, at age twenty, was selected as a deputy by John Slaughter, the newly-elected sheriff of Cochise County, Arizona. Slaughter had witnessed Alvord in action when the young lad was challenged by a local Tombstone tough called "Six-Shooter Jimmy".

Both men had gone for their guns and Alvord won with one deliberately-aimed shot. Alvord worked as Slaughter's backup man in a number of shootouts with outlaws, rustlers and gunmen of all kinds.

On one trip, in 1888, Alvord accompanied Sheriff Slaughter and another deputy, Cesario Lucero in pursuit of three Mexican train robbers. They tracked the men to their camp in the Whetstone Mountains.

The lawmen found their quarry sound asleep in their blankets around a smoldering campfire. The bandits were ordered to surrender. Instead, the outlaws dove for their guns, starting a pitched battle in which one outlaw was shot. When the first train robber fell from his injury, the other two surrendered.

Just a month later, Alvord helped his boss capture three more Mexican bandits. They again crept up on their prey while they were asleep.

When a gun battle ensued, one of the bandits was killed. Another was wounded. The unharmed man surrendered without a fight. The wounded Mexican managed to escape.

Deputy Alvord's life turned downward. He began drinking too much, often with an outlaw element. On one such binge, he got drunk with two surly cowboys in a private house near Sheriff Slaughter's residence.

One of the cowboys objected to a remark of the other cowboy. He grabbed Alvord's gun and shot the other to death. Alvord was too drunk to stop the shooting. When Sheriff Slaughter learned that his deputy's gun had been used in the killing, he exploded, chastising the deputy in front of dozens of witnesses.

Slaughter put the deputy on notice; either he mended his ways or he would be an unemployed lawman. The sheriff said later that the one big mistake in his career was hiring Burt Alvord as his chief deputy. In later years, the mere mention of Alvord's name infuriated Slaughter.

When Alvord continued his wastrel ways of drinking and cavorting with known criminals, the town fathers called for his resignation.

He moved on to Wilcox, Arizona, and took a job as town constable. He still drank heavy and most of the young outlaws labeled him a hopeless alcoholic from whom they had nothing to fear.

One such outlaw was Billy King, a rough and tumble cowboy who started creating trouble in Wilcox one day. Alvord accosted him and ordered him to put away his gun and to stop racing his horse up and down the main street.

Billy King asked Alvord to join him in drinks at the bar to talk things over. After belting down a couple of drinks, King grew sullen and threatening, asking Alvord to join him outside.

As King went through the back door of the saloon, Alvord drew his pistol and fired every bullet in his gun into King's face, killing him.

Alvord gave up the peace-keeping business and turned to a profitable career as a train and bank robber. He led a bunch of train robbers for some years. He was arrested in 1900 and then again in 1903. He and his sidekick, Billy Stiles, were both imprisoned.

Stiles worked his way into a trustee's position at the Tombstone jail and stole the keys to the jail cells. He set Alvord free.

Alvord then decided the best way for he and Stiles to stay free was to play dead. They either killed two Mexicans or unearthed them from recent graves. They sent the bodies to Tombstone in sealed coffins, spreading the word that the pine boxes contained the bodies of Alvord and Stiles.

The ruse didn't work. Suspicious lawmen opened the coffins and found the decaying bodies of the Mexicans. Arizona Rangers pursued Alvord and Stiles into Mexico, ignoring international law. The two outlaws were found in a camp at Nigger Head Gap, Mexico.

Alvord and Stiles both went for their guns and both were wounded in the shootout. Alvord was shot twice in the leg and Stiles received an arm wound. Stiles ran for his horse and raced wildly out of the camp. Alvord, however, was immobilized.

The Rangers arrested him and he was sent to the Arizona prison in Yuma for two years. He was released in 1906. Finally, he traveled to the West Indies and disappeared from history.

CHAPTER 29

THE COLT REVOLVER

'It was better for shooting from horseback'

(Google Images)

It is argued that Colonel Samuel Colt's invention of the Colt Revolver in 1836 revolutionized the West. Colt was from Hartford, Connecticut

Prior to Colt's invention, all handguns were basically single-action weapons of the flintlock or percussion cap variety. There were some odd variations with two barrels, and one multi-firing revolver-type gizmo called the "pepperbox".

Colt's first revolver was a six-shooter of .34 caliber with a four-and-a-half inch barrel. An unguarded trigger dropped down when its handler cocked the gun. There

181

was no big demand for the gun, but a number of them did find their way into Texas and into the hands of the newly-formed Texas Rangers.

The Rangers found them better adapted for fighting on horseback than any of the alternatives. Still, it was considered a flawed instrument.

It was too lightweight and fragile, and in order to reload, it had to be broken down into three pieces and the empty cylinder exchanged for a full one.

This was difficult to do from the back of a galloping horse and Colt failed to see a stampede develop by the public to acquire his new weapon.

Colonel Samuel Colt
(Google Images)

Colt then collaborated with a Texas Ranger named Samuel Walker, who explained the shortcomings of the Colt Revolver to the inventor. Colt next came up with a new model he called the Walker Colt.

It was heavier, with a visible trigger, a trigger guard, and bigger and better-shaped grip that made it easier and steadier to hold. It could also be loaded without removing and exchanging the cylinder. The bore was increased to .44 caliber, which made a bigger hole in whomever or whatever it penetrated.

It was considered more useful, too, when necessity called for it to be used as a shillelagh, Texas style.

Index

185

About the Author

Alton Pryor has been a writer for magazines, newspapers, and wire services for fifty years. He worked for United Press International in their Sacramento Bureau, handling both printed press as well as radio news.

In Salinas, he worked for the Salinas Californian daily newspaper for five years as editor of Western Ranch and Home, a weekend supplement.

In 1963, he joined California Farmer magazine where he worked as a field editor for 27 years. When that magazine was sold, Alton was forced into temporary retirement.

He gained his interest in California and Western history after selling a number of short 500-word articles on Southern California history. In his research of these stories, he kept finding other stories that interested him but did not fit the particular publication for whom he was then writing. He collected both facts and ideas as he researched, and finally turned them into his first book, "Little Known Tales in California History."

Alton Pryor is now the author of fifteen books.

He is a graduate of California State Polytechnic University, San Luis Obispo, where he earned a Bachelor of Science degree in journalism.

US/History

Lawmen in the old west played a juggling act as far as the law was concerned. It was necessary for a successful lawman to be both tougher and smarter than the outlaw. In reality, the lawman was guilty of committing offenses that would be punishable if committed by the outlaw.

The Earp Brothers were no saints. Marshal Henry Plumber was hanged for crimes he committed while wearing a badge.

Most of the sheriffs and marshals wearing badges also played at gambling, often even owning the gambling concessions in the town saloons. As one would suspect, it was gambling that caused much of the trouble in town. The lawmen found themselves both supporting gambling while controlling angry gamblers.

Most lawmen were good with guns and practiced daily. Being a second late on a draw against a fast outlaw gunman could spell the difference in which man lived.

Western author Alton Pryor has brought a host of western lawmen together in one book.